Visiting
Miss Caples

Visiting Miss Caples

Elizabeth Cody Kimmel

Dial Books / New York

Published by Dial Books
A division of Penguin Putnam Inc.
345 Hudson Street
New York, New York 10014

Library of Congress in Publication Data
Kimmel, Elizabeth Cody.
Visiting Miss Caples/by Elizabeth Cody Kimmel.—1st ed.
p.   cm.
Summary: The elderly shut-in she visits once a week becomes an
unexpected source of friendship and strength for thirteen-year-old Jenna,
and they help each other face and overcome painful aspects of their lives.
ISBN 0-8037-2502-7 (hc trade)
[1. Old age—Fiction. 2. Friendship—Fiction.
3. Schools—Fiction.] I. Title.
PZ7.K56475Vi 2000   [Fic]—dc21   99-27899   CIP

For Mom, with love

Chapter 1

Liv and I had a secret passion for fall for as long as I could remember. Fall was a time to compute the summer's full results: inches grown, pounds lost or gained, boys newly in favor and out. The beginning of the school year guaranteed a new book bag and pair of shoes, and maybe a haircut to complete the picture. Each September like clockwork we set to the task of reinventing ourselves, Liv attacking my closet ferociously, tossing aside clothing too small, too frayed, or just too yesterday.

I don't have any memories of life before Liv Townsend. My family moved to Fire Hill, Massachusetts, when I was three or four, and she was immediately on the scene, blazing new trails on her Big Wheel that I eagerly followed. Liv was in on anything that mattered in my life. She made things happen. I suppose I could have gone swimming in the quarry without Liv. I would still have liked missing school during the flu epidemic without her. I might even have been able to hold my own against Mrs. Madison, the mean old lady across the street who'd made a career out of making me miserable. But none of it would have been the same.

All the promise of fall echoed in Liv's voice as she began her annual plundering of my closet.

"Eighth grade is going to be the best yet, Jen," she said, tossing turtlenecks furiously into a pile on the floor. "We're practically in high school. We can take control now."

As far as I could see, Liv had been in control all of our lives. But something made me think that she was right. So when Liv pronounced that nobody could make any kind of statement while wearing a turtleneck, I had to agree. Tossing six perfectly good shirts into the Goodwill pile wasn't something my mother would approve of. But Liv's advice had never failed yet, and my mother had been sort of out of it lately. I made a slight fuss, but in the end, every shirt went into the pile, minus a few threads I carefully snipped out and placed in our burn-bag.

Like I said, I love the fall, and building a fire for the burn-bag is definitely one of the season's highlights. We'd performed this little ritual since fifth grade–filling a small bag with bits and pieces of last year, and burning it in a little fire under an old weeping willow tree. This year we were late getting it together, and school had already started. The cold weather had come unusually soon, and the ground beneath our tree had begun to harden. We settled for a miniature bonfire of twigs and newspapers.

"And so we bid farewell to our seventh-grade selves," Liv said solemnly, tying the bag closed with a piece of string. Between my bits of clothing and bookmark collection, Liv's pom-pom socks and hair scrunchies, and every picture we had cut out of last year's box-office heartthrob, the bag was particularly full this year. We knelt side by side as Liv placed the bag in the center of the little pile.

"The past is smoke in the wind," she said, striking a match.

"The past is smoke in the wind," I repeated as we watched the flames lick the bag. The heat from the fire felt good in the fading late afternoon sunlight. The contents of the bag flared briefly, then crumbled into ashes before our eyes.

"I wonder what we'll be burning next year," I said as Liv tossed handfuls of dirt into the fire.

"Maybe there won't be anything to burn," she said, with a wide smile. "Maybe this year we will be absolutely perfect."

"I don't know," I said. "I may at least want to burn my cafeteria card."

"And those shoes," Liv replied, and I threw a small dirt ball at her.

"It seems like classes are going to be all right, though," I said, ducking as Liv tossed a spray of dirt back at me.

"Except for that human-services project," Liv added. "I can't believe they're making us go through with that."

I couldn't possibly have agreed more. Miss Webster, our social studies teacher, had announced that each one of us would be assigned to visit an elderly shut-in once a week, to read out loud. And there were plenty of people to choose from. Some people still called our town Fossil Hill because so many old people live here. It's not as bad as it used to be—when my family moved here, Liv and I were the only kids around for what seemed like miles. Pretty much everyone on our street was over sixty. Widowed old ladies, mostly. It's changed some now, with younger families moving in, but Fire Hill still has more senior citizens than any town in the state. When I was a little kid, old people really scared me, probably because of my frequent run-ins with Mrs. Madison. I knew this "reach out and touch one of them" project wasn't the kind of thing I was likely to do well with.

For the most part, our friends had greeted the news of the human-services project with a mixture of dread and disgust. Watching them wig out over it all would have been funny if I hadn't been so freaked about the whole thing myself.

"This must break, like, fifty laws, or something," Amber had stated as we hunched around our cafeteria table.

"Child labor, or trespassing, or that other one. What's that other one?"

"So can we sue?" asked Meredith, looking hopeful for the first time that day.

Liv shook her head, but kept silent.

"But how can it be against the law, Mer?" I asked, half laughing. "It's like homework. The school is assigning it to us. How can that be illegal?"

"Because," Meredith began with great authority, but no explanation followed.

"Okay," said Amber suddenly. "It's like this. We pay to go to school, right?"

No one responded. I didn't know about my friends, but I'd certainly never kicked in for my education.

"So," she continued, "they also pay people to take care of geritolics, right?"

"Geriatrics," I corrected, grinning at Liv, who grinned back. Amber made the international "whatever" face.

"So basically the school is, like, forcing us to do something the gerilaxatives are supposed to be paying a salary for. Which is a crime, from where I'm standing."

"Uh, you're not standing, babeski," said Liv. "And about that budding law career? Stick to aspiring fashion critic."

"No, this is totally worth exploring," Meredith piped in. "Who knows about this stuff? What about Jessica? She's always talking about her grandfather, the lawyer, and he's totally old, which probably makes him a geri-galactic too—"

"Enough!" Liv said, waving her hands in the air, and Meredith shut her mouth. "We can't do anything about it, but let's at least not talk about it anymore. I'm trying to eat here. Anyway, I've got more delish things to think about, if you know what I mean."

Amber and Meredith pounced on that, and I watched Liv start to tell them about the new boy she'd seen. And that was pretty much the end of the grassroots movement to sue our school for making us read to old people.

Giving up a whole afternoon every week did seem like a lot to ask. And helping senior citizens, that was more my mother's thing.

Still, everybody in our class had to participate, and that included Liv. Somehow, that made it bearable. And that's the way it had always been. Whether it was riding the Super Duper Looper at Hershey Park or even coming down with a serious case of strep throat, if Liv was doing it, I wanted to as well. That's what real friendship is to me. Maybe, at the ripe old age of thirteen, it was the only thing I really knew for certain about myself.

Chapter 2

As the smoky smell of the burn-bag gradually faded away, the specter of the human-services project loomed ever larger. I had been assigned to a Miss E. Caples. Though her name was unfamiliar to me, I examined it with a sense of relief, as I'd begun to fear I might end up with horrible old Mrs. Madison.

We weren't given much in the way of instructions, except that we should arrive promptly at four o'clock each Wednesday, should bring a book of poetry, a *Reader's Digest*, and a current newspaper, and that we should neither expect nor ask to be fed. We were to stay for one hour, reading whatever was requested. We were to remain, at all times, polite and cheerful. It had been carefully explained to me that Miss Caples was a complete shut-in. She hadn't taken a step outside her apartment in five years or something. I was supposed to be sensitive to that, I was told. The whole thing was just sounding worse and worse. Since there was no way out of it, I decided it would be easier to go along and just get it over with. And I knew it was important to my mother. My mom is one of those truly nice people, the kind that spend their free time helping out because they honestly want to. She'd always been involved in charity stuff, until lately, that is. Though we hadn't exactly been talking much recently, she had mentioned our human-services project a couple of times. I knew she just assumed I would participate with happiness. And so, on that first Wednesday in October, I found myself ringing the doorbell of one Miss E. Caples, *Reader's Digest* in hand.

She lived in one of those buildings that used to be a house, but was now divided into apartments. I rang the doorbell marked Caples. There was a shrill buzzing sound, and the front door vibrated slightly. In the dark front hall, I saw a faded number one in flaking gold paint on the door to the left. I took a deep breath and knocked twice, loudly.

Nothing. She couldn't be deaf, because she'd buzzed me in when I rang the outer bell. So I knocked again, even harder this time. Still nada. I stood there feeling vaguely moronic, and thunked my fist on the door in irritation. The door swung inward with a slight creak. This startled me, and I glanced down the hallway, feeling almost guilty, like I was breaking in. I gave the door a little shove, opening it wider, and took a tentative step inside.

"Hello?" I called. My voice sounded weird and young, not how I liked to imagine I sounded. "It's Jenna from Fire Hill School. Anyone home?"

There was no spoken response, but I heard something. Just a general kind of sound someone might make. A rustle, or a sigh. I was standing in a short, narrow hallway. Ahead, I could see that it opened up into a room. Taking a deep breath, I walked down the hallway and into what looked like the living room. The first thing I noticed was the smell of dust. The second thing I noticed was the photographs.

They were all over the place. Some hanging from the walls, some on tables and other surfaces. Old photographs. They were mostly of people, though I glimpsed some houses and animals. Old-style cars. Groups of women. Everything you can imagine. Like her entire life, or somebody's, was there on display. It was pretty bizarre.

I heard the same, unidentifiable noise as before, and that's when I saw her. She was sitting in an armchair by the window. Her face was bony and pinched. Her hands, gripping the arms of the chair, looked like the roots of an ancient tree. She just stared off into space, with no expression at all.

"Miss Caples?" I asked. "I'm Jenna. From the school. I'm supposed to read to you."

No response. I tried again.

"Is there anything in particular you want me to read? I brought a *Reader's Digest*. And a newspaper. And some poetry."

Still nothing. I felt the hot beginnings of panic rise in the back of my throat. What should I do? Was she sick? Was she senile? I knew she could speak perfectly well, because my teacher, Miss Webster, told us she had spoken to each participant on the phone. So she could speak, but she was simply choosing not to speak to *me*. She obviously didn't want me here. I should leave. I glanced toward the front door, but my feet didn't move. Somehow, I knew that wouldn't work. Miss Webster would never accept it. I'd just be sent back next week, and it would be all the more humiliating.

Miss Caples was just going to have to be read to, whether she liked it or not. There was an uncomfortable-looking wooden chair against the wall. I sat down in it, opened the *Reader's Digest,* and flipped through the pages.

"Okay, what are you in the mood for? We've got 'Laughter, The Best Medicine.' There's an excerpt from the new Barbra Streisand biography. Or 'Humor in Uniform.' Any of that sound good?"

Same total silence, same blank stare.

"Okay, then, this one looks good. 'Tinky, the Hero Schnauzer: How a Sixteen-Pound Dog Saved My Grandfather from Drowning.' How about that?"

And then I just read it out loud. Fairly slowly, but with animation, or inflection, or whatever you call it. I read the whole account of the dog's heroics, and the interviews with the family members and witnesses. I even held up the picture of Tinky for her to see. She didn't bat an eyelash.

By the time it was all over, and Tinky and the author's grandfather sat wet and shivering on the riverbank with police blankets wrapped around them, I expected some reaction. None followed. So I *really* put some effort into the next story, about a grandmother who had gone undercover as a Sherpa mountain guide in the Himalayas. I finished up with an account of a Missouri schoolteacher who was forced to land a plane while simultaneously administering first aid to the pilot and copilot after a galley explosion. I thought I saw Miss Caples's eyelashes flicker when I got to the part about her reattaching the pilot's arm, but it may have just been the light. And by that time, almost the full hour had passed.

"So, I guess that's it, then," I said, closing the magazine. "It's five o'clock. I need to be going."

Miss Caples was looking in a different direction now. Out the window, or maybe at the curtains.

"I'll be back next week, I guess," I said. "Unless you decide this isn't what you had in mind, or whatever. You could just call Miss Webster at the school then, I guess. And tell her."

I gathered up my stuff as quickly as possible, walked down the little hallway, and opened the front door.

As it was closing, I thought I heard her make a noise— at last. Something like a "harrumph." You know. An irritated, exasperated kind of sound only old people make. I shut the door firmly before I could hear anything else.

It was all too obvious. I was much too cool for this.

Chapter 3

Liv was rolling her eyes as she walked toward me.

"So?" she said as she came into range. "How was yours?"

I was really more concerned at that moment with the fact that I'd dropped a heavily buttered piece of toast onto the silk skirt I was wearing at breakfast.

"Look at this!" I said, gesturing at the island-shaped dark stain with disgust. "I can't believe I just left it there. I didn't have time to find a Stain Stick. It's never going to come out now, is it?"

"Mine is fat as all get-out," Liv said, ignoring my distress. "And she bakes. She had this big plate of ginger-snaps, and she wasn't letting me out of there until I ate every one of them."

"What are we talking about?" I asked.

"Biddy-sitting, zoned-out one. Yesterday, remember? Mine's a fatty. The upside is I didn't have to read to her at all. She just blathered away about this and that until it was time for me to leave."

"You are so lucky," I said as a mental image of Miss Caples's pinched, silent faced loomed into view. "Mine is like a vegetron or something. She never spoke. No hello, no good-bye, nothing. God, she never even looked at me."

"Dump her," said Liv, matter-of-factly. "Tell Miss Webster she's a nut job, and you want a new one."

"Yeah," I said, shifting my book bag to my other shoulder. "Maybe. I figure I'll give it one more week. Actually, it could be a good thing, you know? No small talk, no personal questions. I show up, read, and take off. No complications. No unwanted calories."

Liv shrugged. "Whatever," she said.

We paused at the big intersection, waiting for the light to change. Liv scowled into the distance, and I took the opportunity to examine her amazing face. Since I've known Liv for something like ten years, I was there when her regular kid looks turned into drop-dead beauty. Her baby mop of brown hair had turned into a mass of raven curls over the years. Her beautiful hazel eyes became the crown jewels of her face once she swapped her glasses for contacts. She had grown taller, but her bones had remained tiny and bird-fine. Everything she had worked for her. She was your basic knockout.

Now, I'm no slouch in the looks department either.

My hair is dark red, which I used to hate until I found out that boys think it's exotic. I've got good eyes, a decent mouth, and as far as my body goes, well, developments have been kind to me. Even so, I've still sort of ridden on Liv's coattails. Her star rose pretty quickly once we hit middle school. Within weeks she had clearly established herself as the leader, and I was just lucky enough to be her best friend. There has been stuff along the way that I felt like I had to do, and that I'm not exactly thrilled about. Well, you know—no point being the top dogs unless there are bottom dogs to bite. But that's school, right? Dump or be dumped on.

"Now who's a vegetron?" Liv was saying. "Jen, have you heard a word I said?"

"Sorry," I said. "I'm still kind of freaked out about the whole shut-in project."

Liv made a disgusted noise. "Old people," she said. "They're so . . . old." I nodded sympathetically.

"I've been talking about Alec Burke," she said as we joined the masses congregating on the front steps of the school. This was not unusual. Since we'd been back at school, Liv spent a great deal of time talking about Alec Burke. He was new this year. He might not be the coolest guy in school, and he definitely wasn't the best looking, strictly speaking. But what Liv really found irresistible about Alec was that he didn't turn into a drooling idiot whenever he saw her. Most guys did, even ones in high school. But Alec never seemed to notice there was anything special about Liv, and since he didn't seem to be losing his eyesight, he remained a source of fascination to her. She had to have him. I had no doubt that she'd succeed, one way or another.

"I need a plan," she was saying. "Some kind of structure. A focus point. What about a party?"

"Don't look at me," I said. "You know my situation. Throwing parties is not an option."

"Mmm," she replied, looking dissatisfied. "And I'm still walking on thin ice from the pool party incident."

Liv was referring to an experiment of sorts, performed by some overzealous friends, involving the buoyancy of her parents' pull-out sofa. By the time it was pulled from the bottom of the pool . . . well, it was not a happy scene.

"There's the Halloween dance," I reminded her, and she narrowed her eyes thoughtfully.

"The Halloween dance," she repeated. "Tacky, but it could work. The question is, of course, what do I wear."

As the bell for first class rang, Liv walked up the steps, deep in an Alec-induced daydream. She would have bumped into people, but they all got out of her way.

Chapter 4

Miss Caples had decided to stare at the colored glass lamp on the desk.

"Hot off the presses," I said, waving the new *Reader's Digest* in the air. "Lucky us, right?"

Now that I knew what to expect, I felt a bit less self-conscious. In fact, as I began my second visit, I still had no indication that Miss Caples even knew I was in the room.

"More stories of heroic cats and dogs," I said enthusiastically, glancing over the table of contents. "Results of the poetry contest. A Native American legend."

I settled on one of the "Brave Pets" accounts. Between you and me, I'm a sucker for those. I didn't look up from the magazine until I'd finished the whole story. A cat had appeared from somewhere, and had settled into

Miss Caples's lap. It was one of those black-and-white jobs, the shorthaired kind. I am definitely not a cat person, but if I have to be around one, I prefer the shorthaired ones to those longhaired things with the pushed in faces—the kind you see on the gourmet cat food commercials, eating mousse-de-salmon out of a crystal bowl. But this cat looked harmless enough, and I noticed one of Miss Caples's twisted hands had strayed over the cat's back, and was now pressing into his fur. So she could move, anyway.

I glanced at my watch and noted the time. Still fifteen minutes to go, and my reading energy was just about exhausted. Wondering what to do, I noticed a teacup and saucer on the table next to Miss Caples's chair.

"Um, can I take those into the kitchen for you?" I asked, a little nervously.

"I could, you know, wash them for you, if you wanted," I said. When she didn't answer, I got up and walked over to the table beside her. She didn't move at all. The cat raised his head, though, and stared at me with huge green eyes.

"Hi there, kitty," I said, picking up the cup and saucer carefully.

There were even photographs in the kitchen. I examined them as I washed the dishes. Some of the faces were becoming familiar. There was a beautiful young woman who appeared in a lot of the pictures, often alongside a tall man with piercing eyes. I couldn't have said exactly when the pictures were taken, but they all had that really old feel about them. You know, like before most everything cool was invented. I examined the teacup's fading rose pattern for a moment, wondering how old it was and how many thousands of servings of tea it had held. Placing both cup and saucer gently on the counter, far enough from the edge so the cat wouldn't accidentally knock them to the floor, I walked back into the living room.

"Okay, so the cup and saucer are clean. I just left them on the counter. I should probably get going, I guess."

I'd developed the habit of not looking at Miss Caples when I spoke to her, partly because it embarrassed me, and partly because she wasn't looking at me either, so I didn't think it mattered. I couldn't help sneaking a little peek, though, when I'd finished speaking. Her lips looked tight. What, she was mad at me now? I shook my head slightly. Maybe Liv was right. I should just tell Miss Webster my shut-in was a nut job, and have done with it.

"Okay," I said, backing down the hallway. "So, you know. Bye, or whatever."

So without further fanfare, I quietly shut Miss Caples's door behind me.

Chapter 5 *Elspeth*

She came again today, with her fancy clothes and her Reader's Digest. Reader's Digest, *my eye. Probably all she's capable of reading. Not like we were at that age. We knew who we were. We respected our elders. Didn't shunt our old people aside like yesterday's mending. Nowadays, you pass a certain age in life, you stop being a person and start being just an old person. That's what she thinks. No manners. Won't even look at me when she speaks. Thinks old people don't deserve common courtesy. That we're all senile, probably. That we don't notice things like that.*

Well, those busybodies at Social Services can make me let her in every week, but they can't make me talk to her. They can't make me look at her either, not that she'd notice. Wouldn't you know they'd send me this rude girl. Life has a way of punishing you, I guess, in a hundred different ways. Making me endure this rude girl with a pile of red hair every Wednesday is just the latest.

And what was she doing touching my china? A child like that doesn't understand a thing about bone china. My great-grandmother brought that whole set over with her on the boat from Scotland. Hand packed each piece in linen. She didn't go to all that trouble just to have some heavy-handed redhead toss the teacups around. She hadn't any right to touch them. She ought *to have known better.*

I could just call Social Services or that school myself, tell them to stop her from coming. I only agreed to try it. Never said anything about sticking with it. And if she's going to behave this way, almost breaking my precious heirlooms, and making fun of my cat . . . Well, that wasn't part of the bargain. But what can you expect from one of these thoughtless modern teenagers? I should have known the minute she walked through the door.

I'll call them, then. I'll tell them to send her away. That I don't want to see her, I don't want to know about her. I have enough trouble with my memories.

I'll tell them next week.

Chapter

We were sitting in her bedroom, drinking tall glasses of diet root beer, when it started. As her parents' raised voices easily reached our ears, Liv fell silent, her lips pressed tightly together. The grin had faded immediately from her face, and the joke she'd started telling me was left unfinished.

Mr. Townsend was always at home, because he had his own business. Something about real estate, I know, but it was supposed to be fancier than the regular kind. I got the idea he was like a mogul-in-training, or something. Big wheel. Hot shot. Those were the words I'd heard my parents use to describe him, anyway. I'd even heard him use them to describe himself.

But he wasn't working now. He was yelling at the top of his lungs, and Mrs. Townsend was yelling just as loudly. I'd never heard them fight. They were the kind of people who thought appearances were the most important thing in the world. Liv used to say they spent so much time making sure they looked happy, they didn't have any time left over to actually *be* happy. Truthfully, I never was all that fond of either of Liv's parents. Her dad was always working, or yakking on the phone, or talking about how much money he'd made on his last deal. And her mom was kind of a snob. I guess Liv had her snobby moments too, but it wasn't the same. Anyway, so I didn't have warm feelings for Mr. or Mrs. Townsend, but this was the first time I had felt uncomfortable in the house because of them. Liv just stared into her ice.

There was a slam. We heard footsteps, and the door to Liv's room opened. Her mother, red-faced, took a step inside.

"Well, you can forget about the riding lessons," she said. "And Florida too. If you have a problem with that, talk to the tycoon. This is his doing, not mine."

She didn't wait for a response, and she didn't acknowledge me with so much as a glance. The door closed with a click, and the footsteps faded. Liv was shaking her head back and forth in a tiny, silent no. Finally, she looked up at me.

"You might as well know," she said, with an almost blank expression. "The checkout girl at the Dairy-Mart and her brother Sam will probably know by the end of the month. It's money. My dad's business. He made some kind of . . . mistake or something. And now everybody is calling him on his loans, or his borrowings or whatever, and the tax guys are threatening him."

I didn't know what to say. Did she mean her dad was broke?

"So as you can see," she said, raising her hands in the air, "I've lost my chance to train as an Olympic riding champion. I will not be getting a savage tan in Florida this Christmas, and my hopes of filling my closet with the latest and greatest are way over."

I knew I should say something.

"Is there anything . . . I mean, couldn't you get help or something? Maybe my parents could lend your dad—"

Liv cut me off with an icy look.

"We are *not* planning on becoming one of your mother's charity cases. God, Jen, be real. I'm just saying he's having a really bad year, business-wise. We're not, like, going under or anything. Don't blow this out of proportion."

Liv changed the subject by plunking a video into her VCR and hitting rewind. If only I could rewind the entire afternoon and record something else over it, I thought. Something light, and funny. With no shouting.

Chapter 7

The next day we filed out of bio lab and into the rapidly filling hallway.

"Lockers, babe-o-la," Liv said, motioning for me to follow her.

She hadn't mentioned anything about her parents, the fight, or anything. I was beginning to think that maybe I had just made too much of it.

I hardly noticed the sea of faces as we made our way down the hall. People were waving, and calling out greetings, and I must have made some kind of mechanical response.

"God, I hate Tuesdays. So was that a pathetic spectacle, or what?" Liv asked, as she reached for her combination lock with a perfectly manicured hand.

"Which one?" I asked, suddenly at attention. "There are so many."

Liv laughed. "The dissection deal in bio," she said. "Heinous Janeus."

Jane Walsh was, according to Liv, one of the "Primary Reasons For All Pain" in our universe. Heinous Janeus, as Liv liked to call her, was an eighth grader, same as us. I wouldn't call her officially fat, just maybe a bit chunky. She was about average height, with long, baby-fine hair of a nondescript color. Her skin was pale and her eyes were enormous. In the official social system, Jane ranked in both the Brain and the Nerd sections. Jane was always making contributions to the school paper, and doing other "I Live to Serve" things of that type. Plus, she was a Granola Eater, meaning she was into all those earth causes, the tree and animal things. You know, always passing out leaflets or trying to get people to sign her petitions. She really hadn't changed since fourth grade, but somehow she hadn't been such a source of annoyance back then. We'd even played together in those days. But now her causes drove us crazy. She was especially wild for anything having to do with animals, which became a problem in bio today, since we're just weeks away from the highly anticipated frog dissection.

"It's just so lame," Liv was saying. "All she's trying to do is call attention to herself with all that 'conscientious objections' crap."

"Yeah," I said, looking down the hallway. "Still, if she

gets Mr. Wood to cancel the dissection, that would be cool. I don't exactly want to do it either."

"You don't want to do it because it's gross," said Liv. "Which is normal. You're not making it into some pathetic cause. It's a frog, for God's sake. Who cares?"

"I know," I said, nodding. "And here's our friend now."

Jane was wearing one of those Indian skirt things, and sandals with socks. Exactly the kind of clothing that really bugs the hell out of Liv. As she got closer to us, Liv slammed her locker shut and turned in Jane's direction, narrowing her beautiful eyes to slits.

"What's with the floor-length skirt, Heinous? Forget to shave your legs again?"

Jane reached into her locker without looking at either of us. Liv glanced at me.

"You're looking a little green, Jane," I called out. "Frog got your tongue?"

Liv gave a delighted giggle.

"Not too happy about the upcoming slice and dice class?" I continued. "The froggie won't feel it, you know. You stick a pin into its little brain to knock it out. Of course, I suppose you'd never really know if the little thing could feel you slicing it open or not, eh? I mean, frogs can't scream, right?"

Jane slammed her locker closed, threw me an angry look, and hurried down the hall without comment. Liv was almost beside herself with laughter.

"Oh God, Jenna, that was perfect!"

I guess that was one word for it. It was just so easy,

you know? With Jane in particular. She practically begged for it. I guess she was harmless enough in her own way, but sometimes I looked at her and just felt angry. Why did she seem to go out of her way to stick out, especially when she knew people would make fun of her? I guess if Jane wanted to irritate people, that was her right, but she'd have to live with the consequences.

The thing was, Liv seemed to be dishing it out more, or enjoying it more, this year. I mean, there were always people on her diss list. She was beautiful, and popular, and she made the most of it. Who wouldn't? But this month, I could name four girls I personally witnessed Liv reduce to tears. For no real reason. And I always joined in, because that was just what you did. And it was fun, or whatever. To be looked up to, you know. To have people want to sit next to you, or get out of your way in the cafeteria. I have to say, I never minded that.

Chapter **8**

"Sit up straight," said my mother, her back to me as she stared out the kitchen window at the growing dark.

"Why?" I asked. "There's no one here but us, and you're not even looking at me. What difference does it make if my spine is straight while I'm eating?"

"Sit up straight," she repeated.

It's something like this pretty much every night now. My father is one of those high-powered corporate workaholic types, so we don't see much of him. He leaves at the crack of dawn, and when he does get home, he's so spent, he usually just collapses on the couch with his *Wall Street Journal* and his gin and tonic. No one's allowed to make *any* noise.

So this leaves me having a cozy, intimate dinner by myself at the kitchen table, while my mother stares out of the window and tells me to put my napkin in my lap, or to push my hair out of my eyes. There was a time when dinner used to be a real event in our house. My mother can cook up a storm when she wants to. Even when my father wasn't home in time to eat with us, dinner was always something I'd looked forward to. Mom and I would stuff ourselves, then sit surrounded by dirty plates, joking and gossiping. We hadn't had one of those leisurely dinners in a long time. A really long time.

"The Jeep's got to go to the garage for a tune-up," she said, to no one in particular.

I speared a hunk of roast chicken on my fork. My mother turned from the window to face me.

"It's the kind of thing that's got to be taken care of on schedule," she said. I nodded, figuring she must know what she was talking about, even if I didn't.

I watched her pick up the phone, dial, and ask for my father. I started thinking about Heinous Janeus for some reason, picturing her at a kitchen table in some house on the other side of town, eating her granola dinner and worrying about a bunch of stupid frogs. Just thinking about that pale, chunky weirdo and her righteous causes started getting me irritated.

My mother's voice took on a strange quality.

"I don't understand," she was saying into the phone. "I thought he . . . When did he leave?"

My thoughts did an abrupt shift and a bad feeling seeped into my stomach.

"Well, did he leave a number?" she asked, her expression getting darker.

I jumped as she slammed the phone onto the cradle with a bang.

"Mom? Did . . . is everything okay?"

"Everything's fine, Jen, eat your dinner," she said quickly. The words were normal enough, but she spoke like a robot. "I'll have to speak to him later. After he–" She just stopped talking, then, and I stood up.

"Mom, what did they say?" I asked, my voice wavering.

"Eat your dinner, Jen!" she snapped. "I've got things to take care of. I can't–just eat your dinner. I'll be up-stairs."

She hadn't said a word that meant anything, but she didn't have to. I knew what was going on. It was hap-pening all over again.

The last time was exactly two years ago. Suddenly my father wasn't in his office when he was supposed to be, and my mother would get that strange look when she tried to call him. As far as I know, she never knew ex-actly who the other woman was, and after a while, the whole thing just seemed to stop. But everything was different. Suddenly my mother started spending dinner-time staring out of the window, and giving me meaning-less suggestions about my hair and posture. Their arguing was replaced by a silence that seemed to suck every bit of life out of our house.

I had really hoped that once enough time had passed, things would start to get better. Tonight made it clear that wasn't going to happen. My throat felt thick, and my eyes hot. As I stared at my plate, the phone rang, startling me.

I got to it as quickly as I could, answering it before it could ring a second time. It was better that I handle it, for now. Let my father make his worthless explanation to me. But it was Liv.

"Would you believe," she began, plunging right in, "that Ellis Green's moldy-oldy actually croaked this morning of a heart attack? Can you even imagine? Of course, if I had to listen to Ellis Green read to me in that nasal voice every week, I might die too. But do you think she's going to get, like, credit for this? Or is she going to have to get a new wrinkloid, and start all over again? Jen? Are you there?"

A big sob forced its way out of my throat. There was the briefest of pauses, then Liv spoke again.

"Under our tree, babe-o-la," she said. "Three minutes." She hung up, because she didn't need to say anything else. I paused only to dump the remains of my dinner in the trash, and drop my plate into the sink.

By the time I was out the front door, a few fat raindrops had begun to blot the sidewalk. Liv was already jogging up the street toward our willow tree. She came toward me, breathing a little quickly from her run, her brow furrowed with concern.

"What happened, Jen?" she said, and at the sound of the genuine sweetness in her voice, I dissolved into tears big time.

"He's doing it again," I got out between sobs. "She

called his office, he wasn't . . . Why does he do it, Liv? Why?"

As the rain beat down harder, Liv wrapped her arms around me, and pressed her head against mine.

"Cry it out, sweetie," she whispered. "Then we'll handle it. We can handle anything, remember?"

So I cried under the willow, and I hung on to Liv, who had suddenly become the old Liv, the way she was before she was so beautiful and the world crouched at her feet.

Chapter 9

Jane Walsh was coming down the hall with a stack of flyers in one hand and a roll of tape in the other. She gave
me a wide berth, and I didn't even try to talk to her. I
had more important things on my mind anyway. My father had come home very late the night before, and if he
and my mother had had any kind of discussion, I
couldn't hear it. Still, I hadn't completely lost interest in
my surroundings, so I reached out and grabbed one of
the flyers off of the wall. The headline screamed:

STOP NEEDLESS TORTURE AND SLAUGHTER OF ANIMALS

The murder of animals to satisfy the whims of
a biology class is UNACCEPTABLE.

It is in NO way crucial to our scientific curriculum to
personally vivisect and view the inner organs of
an innocent creature. This callous misuse of animal life
is MORALLY REPREHENSIBLE.

Join me and REFUSE to participate in the
scheduled November frog dissection in eighth-grade
biology. DEMAND that the exercise be replaced with
an activity that does not infringe on any kind of life.

SILENCE EQUALS ACCEPTANCE—SO SPEAK UP!!!

I was about to mush the flyer up into a ball and throw it
away when I noticed Alec Burke coming down the hall
toward me, a copy of the flyer in his hand. He was reading Jane's little statement and scowling, or maybe he was
just concentrating. I didn't have real feelings about Alec
Burke one way or the other, but my loyalty to Liv made
it impossible for me to let him by without getting a word
in on her behalf.

"Hey, Alec," I said in a casual way. "Frogs, huh?" I
pointed at the flyer. *Duh,* I thought as soon as the words
were out of my mouth.

"You gonna do it?" he asked.

"Of course," I replied emphatically. "Me and Liv
both." It was only after I'd answered him that I realized
I wasn't sure if 'do it' referred to the dissection, or the
boycott.

"Good," he said with a grin. "Great. Me too."

He pushed past me without another word, leaving me

wondering exactly what it was I'd committed Liv and myself to.

I explained this to her as gently as possible during lunch.

"Oh, he meant the dissection," she said, her mouth partially full of sandwich.

"That's what I figured," I said, "but then I realized he hadn't *really* said, one way or the other."

"Trust me," she replied. "Alec is no Granola Boy. His parents drive a Jag, remember? And I've seen his mom—she's a total fur hound."

I nodded.

"So tell me again what you said," Liv said intently. "Word for word."

"He asked if I was going to do it, and I said, 'Oh, sure. Me and Liv both.'"

Liv gave an approving nod.

"Good," she said. "And he came back with . . ."

"He said, 'Great, so am I.' And he smiled."

"A big smile?" she pressed. "A meaningful smile?"

To be honest, I really didn't know what Liv's definition of a meaningful smile was. But I wanted her to be happy.

"I'd call it meaningful," I said, and Liv beamed.

"Excellent work, girlfriend," she said. "With your help, he will be *miiiiine.*"

I smiled back at Liv, and hoped it was true.

"Want to take the long way home this afternoon?" I asked, and Liv shook her head.

"It's Wednesday, remember? Fossil-sitting day," she said.

I groaned. I'd completely forgotten about it, and hadn't brought any reading material with me. Between my situation at home, and the whole frog drama at school, Miss Caples and her silent world seemed a million miles away.

Chapter 10

"So I was confused about which day it was," I explained. "So I kind of forgot the *Reader's Digest*. I hope that's not a total disappointment for you."

Miss Caples examined the rug with a vengeance.

"I was thinking maybe you had something around here you'd like me to read," I continued. "A novel, or a newspaper maybe?"

A quick glance around the living room was not encouraging. There had to be something. Probably tucked neatly away in an ancient cabinet. I stood up to get a better look, and my eyes turned to the photographs.

"These are great pictures," I said, examining a small group on the side table. There were several pictures of the girl I'd seen before. Miss Caples didn't seem to be paying attention at all, so I picked one of the pictures up.

"This one again, huh? You've got a lot of pictures of her. She totally looks like a movie star."

I squinted to get a better look. The black-and-white tones of the picture had faded, but there was still a great deal of detail. She was with another girl, a bit shorter than she was, in this picture. They were standing in front of an old stone building, their arms around each other's waists. The movie star girl was wearing a drab outfit that had to be a uniform, and she held a floppy hat in one hand. The uniform was a simple, light shirt and V-necked sweater over a long, pleated skirt. Below the hemline the girls' legs were covered by dark stockings, and they wore light-colored boots. The glamour girl's uniform seemed too big. The huge sweater hung on her, shapeless. In sharp contrast to the sacklike clothing, the girl's face was delicate yet vivid. Unique. Her mouth was open in a laughing smile, and her hair was blowing wildly in the wind. It was darker than blond—maybe honey colored. Or maybe the photo had just faded. But there was nothing faded about that face. She was maybe the most beautiful girl I had ever seen.

Her friend was smaller, and her uniform fit a lot better. She was pretty, but nowhere near as brilliant-looking as her friend. Her expression was more serious, and her face more thoughtful. I wondered who she was. I couldn't remember the girl's face from any of the dozens of pictures in Miss Caples's apartment.

I had been holding the picture in one hand to get a better look at it. Aware suddenly that I'd had it for some time, I put it back on the table, and turned to some of the other photographs. One showed a group of adults standing at the mouth of a cave. Another was of a dark-haired woman in front of an old-style car. In a little silver frame was another shot of the stunning girl in that same baggy uniform. I picked it up. It was very similar to the first picture, except her smile was less spontaneous-looking, somehow more deliberate. I squinted at the background. Was it a school of some kind? There was a cross visible in the window—a church?

I heard a slight rush of air behind me, a breathing out, and I replaced the photograph quickly, and turned around.

"Sorry," I said. "I got kind of lost in your pictures there, for a minute."

Suddenly, Miss Caples turned her head ever so slightly in my direction and gave a small nod. Then, before I had time to catch her eye, she resumed her turned away, glassy stare, her skinny chest rising and falling quietly beneath her faded dress.

But something had changed. The dynamic, as Miss Webster would have called it, had changed.

"I just couldn't find anything to read to you, that's all," I explained, hoping for another reaction. Not this time.

I adjusted the photographs slightly on the table, then pulled my usual uncomfortable wooden chair a bit closer to where Miss Caples was sitting.

"Well," I said finally, taking a seat. "Since I can't read

to you, I guess I'll tell you a story instead. A true one, about my biology class and this really gross experiment we're supposed to do."

And as Miss Caples breathed in and out, and the cat purred, and the black-and-white faces stared out at me from their tarnished frames, I recounted the story of the frogs, and Jane and her flyers, and Alec Burke, and Liv. I didn't leave a single detail out. And that was the first time that I stayed at Miss Caples's past five o'clock.

Chapter **11** *Elspeth*

1933. St. Mary's School for Girls. And stop putting your greasy fingerprints all over it! Don't know why you care, anyway. It's nothing to you. It's nothing to anyone, anymore.

Those Sisters couldn't make a uniform ugly enough to stunt her looks. Heaven knows they tried. Look how baggy the sweater is. How it hangs on her. Covering a multitude of sins, they'd say. And hiding her away with all us good little Catholic girls. As if that would have made a difference. It's almost comical now—it would have been then too, if things hadn't turned out the way they did. What did the poet say—the one who coughed himself to death so young? "Beauty is truth, truth beauty." Back then, I believed in that with all my heart. Surely such heart-stopping beauty must be a blessing, an outward confirmation of true goodness? And I wasn't the only one who thought so. Everyone worshiped her. But she chose me.

Going on about frogs! As if that means anything. It's not frogs you're talking about, that's as plain as day. You're talking about something else, even if you don't know it. Something deeper. Something dangerous. Something I know about.

Chapter **12**

When I got home, I saw my father's car in the driveway. This was not something that happened often on a week-day before dinner.

Usually I would seek refuge at Liv's, but since The Afternoon, I got the feeling Casa Townsend was somewhat off-limits. My house wasn't any more inviting. As I rubbed my cold nose, I decided I'd rather freeze outside than in my own home.

Tossing my backpack onto the front steps, I walked down the driveway and stood by the side of the road, thinking. Across the street, Mrs. Madison's old house loomed darkly against the sky.

From what people said, the old woman had money enough. Why didn't she paint the place? The house was like her–ugly, a shambles. Mrs. Madison had been my sworn enemy for as long as I could remember. She used to call my parents when I was a kid playing around on my bike, complaining that I was using her driveway. Which I was, but so what? Liv and I used to bike as fast as we could up a small slope of road, turn around in her driveway, then race back down the hill. She called us on it every time. Said we were trespassing. It still kills me to think about it—this old lady sitting at her window waiting for these little girls to turn their bikes into her driveway so she could complain about it. The sign came later. DO NOT TURN IN DRIVEWAY, painted in big black letters. It's still there.

And there were a hundred other things you could get into trouble for without even stepping foot onto her property. Staring. That was one of them. According to Mom, Mrs. Madison used to call the police to say people were staring at her house. Oh, and theft of water! I had one of those big plastic kiddy swimming pools, and when my mom would turn on the hose to fill it up, Mrs. Madison would start screaming at us that we were stealing her water. I guess she's always been a total lunatic.

Still, Mom insisted on doing stuff for her. Checking on her when the power went out, leaving fruitcake in her mailbox at Christmas, things like that. She's always reminding me that Mrs. Madison is an old lady living all alone, and that I shouldn't judge her too harshly.

As I stood at the edge of my driveway, rubbing my arms against the cold, I heard a car coming, and just knew it was her. Mrs. Madison had to be in her late eighties, at least, and she still drove her own car. It had those fin things on the back, like they had in the fifties or sixties. My father used to try and guess how much the car was worth, because she always kept it in pretty good condition. Maybe my father entertained fantasies that he could get his hands on the car after Mrs. Madison died. But I didn't think people like Mrs. Madison ever died.

I just stood where I was, one hand on our mailbox, as her car came toward me at a crawl. She slowed almost to a stop next to our driveway, and then peered through the window at me, her face in a tight, suspicious scowl. Her hair was that old-person generic color, her lips small and tight under a messy blob of lipstick. Her mouth was moving, like she might be saying something to me, or muttering to herself. This went on for about one very long minute, and then she hit the gas and cruised up her driveway.

"Lunatic," I mumbled, frustrated that she could still bother me.

I turned quickly at the sound of another car door slamming closed, and an engine starting. My father's car backed quickly down the driveway. I just got a glimpse of him behind the wheel—a blur in an expensive suit. He turned onto the road and drove off. I looked back at my house. Upstairs, a light flicked on. It seemed more like an accident than any real sign of life.

Chapter 13

I can't honestly say it was ever perfect. But it was much better, once upon a time, before Dad made vice president, then senior vice president, then executive senior big guy whatever he is now.

We had a life together back then. And he had a life that wasn't completely consumed by business. My dad loved to swim—in college he'd won all these trophies, which he used to keep in the den. He'd even let me play with them sometimes, like they were dolls. It was kind of funny, actually, piling all these fake gold statues of men in Speedos into my dollhouse. But then one day he gathered all those trophies and packed them away. That was years ago.

You're supposed to love your father, and I suppose I do love mine. But I can't say we were ever actually friends. He never took walks with me, or taught me to play ball or ride a bike, or really seemed like he felt comfortable spending time with me, just the two of us.

Except for this one time. It was when we used to take a cottage up at Cape Cod for two weeks each summer. He'd be there for most of it. This particular summer, I don't remember how old I was, he decided to teach me to swim. It took almost the whole two weeks we were there, but he did it. Taught me how to keep my head above the water and get somewhere without swallowing half the ocean. That might have been the last summer he stayed for the whole two weeks. After a couple years, he'd only come to the Cape on weekends, then he stopped coming at all. Said he couldn't afford to miss those deals—that there was always some other guy who'd use the time to get ahead of him. So he stayed ahead and kind of left us behind in the process.

Chapter 14

"She's going to do something in class on Friday," Liv announced. "We need to be ready."

"How do you know?" I asked, glancing around the cafeteria.

"I heard from someone who went to her stupid meeting," Liv replied, flattening a milk carton. "She's going to make some big pitiful statement, and ask everybody who supports her to stand up too. She got Mr. Wood to say he'd stand outside during the vote so people wouldn't be worried about it affecting their grades, or whatever. He wouldn't do it until Principal Dodson okayed it, but still, can you believe it? Only Miss Totally Responsible could get a teacher to actually agree to leave his own class. Ellis says Jane's been calling people and chasing them down for days, trying to get them on her side."

"She hasn't said anything to me," I said, stabbing at my Jell-O with a plastic spoon.

"Well, duh," Liv said, rolling her eyes. "She's like, terrified of us, remember? And she should be," she added with a smirk. "She's pathetic. I plan to make life very, very unpleasant for our dear Frog Freak."

Her face filled with a sly grin, and I was torn between a feeling of pleasure that she seemed happy, and surprise at the heightened quality of beauty Liv's face acquired when she was plotting someone's downfall. As I studied her face, her calculating smile suddenly disappeared, and was replaced with something resembling anxiety.

"Alec alert," she muttered under her breath. "Heading this way. Ask him to sit with us, Jen. I'm not going to notice him or even look up until you say something."

Studying the contents of her tray, Liv rearranged her hair with a well-practiced toss of her head. The only times Liv ever seemed like a regular, normal person these days was when Alec was approaching. Since school had started, she'd picked up this kind of superior air. Maybe it was a defensive thing. Some of her dad's clients had kids in our school, and rumors were spreading about his financial problems. No one said anything directly to Liv, but she had to know.

Liv lost her supreme confidence and sense of superiority when Alec was around, and she'd start wondering mundane things, like whether she had spinach on her teeth, or if her breath was all right. I have to admit, I secretly kind of liked it.

"Is he looking?" she whispered, and as I shook my head, she quickly tossed her cup of Jell-O onto my tray.

"Can't be seen with that," she murmured. "It gives the wrong impression."

Never mind what impression was given by the fact that I now had two Jell-O cups on my tray. I tracked Alec without actually looking at him, until I sensed he was within several feet of our table.

"Alec, hey," I said with a smile. "What's up? Sampling today's mystery meat? Don't keep us in suspense—we're dying to know what it is."

Alec hesitated for a moment, and looked past me, like he'd intended to sit somewhere else. I was acutely aware of Liv's silence next to me. Quickly extending my leg under the table, I nudged the empty chair out a few feet.

"Sit thee down," I said.

He gave another glance past me, then plunked his tray down on our table with a tiny shrug. Liv chose this moment to notice he'd arrived.

"Alec, whoa," she said with a brilliant smile. "How long have you been standing there?"

Liv had this way of making most people feel like they were standing around waiting for her to notice them.

"I've got to scarf this down pronto," he said, sitting down and indicating his lunch with a nod of his head. "I'm supposed to be somewhere five minutes ago."

A brief, uncomfortable silence followed. Liv pinched my leg under the table.

"So what's been going on?" I asked, fixing Alec with what I hoped was a partially disinterested stare.

"Where?" he asked, his mouth partially full of sloppy joe.

"I don't know," I said. "With you, or whatever."

"Same old, same old," he replied, taking another generous bite.

"So this whole biology class thing is pretty sad," I pressed, and Alec looked up with interest.

"You're telling me," he said. Sensing safe ground, Liv seized the opportunity.

"What is it with people, anyway?" she said. "Why is this even, like, an issue? Or whatever."

"You are so right, Liv," Alec replied through chews. "Good point. The fact that it's even an issue says a lot."

"It's pathetic," Liv continued. "It makes me sick."

"Then I hope you're going to say something," Alec said.

"I totally intend to say something," Liv said with conviction. "I mean, please. It's like, how hard is it to speak, or whatever?"

Alec fixed Liv with an approving look. "Tomorrow, though," he said. "Wait till tomorrow, when she's having her moment."

"Oh yeah," Liv said. "I'm primed to get the most public effect, you know?"

Alec consumed the last remaining contents of his lunch, and rubbed his mouth vigorously with his napkin.

"I'm glad someone isn't afraid to stick to their guns at this school," he said. Liv beamed.

"People are wusses," she said. "Right, Jen?"

"Absolutely," I replied, nodding slightly.

"Gotta hop," Alec said, standing suddenly. "I'm psyched though, for tomorrow. It's gonna be real."

"*Very* real," Liv declared.

"Later," he added, turning on his heel and trotting toward the exit.

Liv turned to me, glowing.

"How awesome was that?" she asked.

"Way awesome," I replied.

"He totally likes me," she said.

"It's certainly beginning to look that way," I replied. "He didn't say two words to me. It was all you."

Liv nodded with satisfaction.

"This is *so* perfect," she said. "I can publicly humiliate Heinous Janeus and get in good with Alec at the same time! It's delicious!"

Delicious wasn't exactly the word that came to mind. In fact, I was starting to feel a little uncomfortable with the Jane thing. I mean, we'd always made fun of Jane. It was just the natural way of things. But Jane hadn't actually done anything wrong, and now Liv was all in a lather planning this thing. This . . . delicious . . . thing. It was leaving a bit of a bad taste in my mouth.

"What are you going to do?" I asked, trying not to sound worried.

"I'm just going to tell her exactly what I think of her," she said. "What *everyone* thinks of her. When she has her big moment, you know, like Alec said. She's going to look like a total moron. Bet she'll cry," she added.

"She will," I said, growing annoyed at the thought of Jane's round face covered with tears.

"Listen, Jen," Liv said suddenly, giving me a no-nonsense look. "This is going to be totally my thing, got it? I'm going to do the talking. I don't want you getting credit for my deal."

"Whatever," I said with a shrug, secretly feeling relieved.

Chapter **15**

"I'd like to make a public statement," Jane was saying, "to ask people who agree with me to make their positions known at this time. Mr. Wood?"

Our teacher stood up and readjusted his glasses. Though his face seemed expressionless, I could tell he was irritated.

"Yes. As I'm sure most of you know, Principal Dodson is allowing Jane to take a vote on the matter of dissection. So that none of you will feel unduly pressured to vote one way or the other on my behalf, I will step into the hallway for a moment. *Five* minutes," he added, glancing at Jane. She nodded gravely.

When he had shut the door behind him, Jane stood and looked around at the students. I could see Liv draw herself slightly up in her seat, rigid with anticipation. Alec's expression was unreadable.

"As you're all aware," Jane began, "this class is scheduled to participate in the killing and dissection of an animal next week. I think most of you know my position on this issue. It comes down to one basic thing: All life is sacred, and deserving of respect. We're being asked to cut open an innocent creature and examine its inner organs. This isn't going to tell us anything we can't learn through other methods. Going about it this way isn't going to help us get into college, or get a good job. It isn't going to expand our world view, or make us better people. Our textbook is full of detailed illustrations of the inner systems of animals, including frogs. The dissection is simply a departure from routine, all to provide a little distraction and amusement for a biology class."

Jane paused, and screwed up her face somewhat.

"That's just wrong, guys. It says something really awful about us that we'd even consider going ahead with it. I guarantee you, in one hundred years kids will hear that animals used to be cut up in school, and they won't be able to believe it. It will be as unthinkable to them as dissecting a human being in class. The only question is when the intolerance starts. I say let's start it now."

She looked around at the class with a serious expression.

"I'd like to know what you think," she said. "And I'd like to know how many—"

"I'll tell you what *I* think, Jane," said Liv, in a dangerously pleasant voice. "May I speak now?"

Jane looked a little scared, but she gave a slight nod.

"Oh good," said Liv with a cold smile. "This is what I think, then. I think you're fat, Jane."

The class erupted with surprised giggles. Liv continued.

"I think you're fat, and I think you have the fashion sense of a bag lady. I think you have strong feelings of inadequacy, and a fear that you don't measure up to the rest of us. My advice to you is to seek professional help. And cut the snacks."

Some people were snickering, and some were just staring at Liv in amazement, mouths hanging open.

"Making some bogus moral claim isn't going to change your status, Jane. I'm sure we all understand your need to feel important, but believe me, you're only making an embarrassment of yourself. Take my advice and sit down, shut your mouth, and don't even think about frogs for the rest of the term. It's better that we just think you're a loser, without you getting up and proving it to everybody."

With that, Liv turned her palms upward and smiled sweetly, indicating she'd finished.

Even I was shocked by the ferocity of Liv's attack. This was the kind of war you waged on someone who had stolen your boyfriend, or ratted you out, or something that really mattered. But Liv was doing this for kicks. Just to see how far she could go. I couldn't look at her. I stared at Jane, instead.

Jane had turned scarlet, and tears were beginning to fill in her eyes. But to my complete surprise, she continued to stand in front of everyone.

"All right," Jane said in a slightly trembling voice. "That's one opinion. I'm not sure how relevant it is to this discussion. . . . Since we don't have a lot of time, I'll just take a head count, and write the results on the board for Mr. Wood. So, whoever agrees with me that the dissection is wrong, if you could just indicate that by standing up."

Some people stood up right away. Some waited to see who stood and who didn't before making their choice. The Brains and Nerds got up en masse. Most of the guys, especially the jocks, remained sitting. Ellis Green got up, and gave Liv and me a nasty look, which was basically meaningless, since Ellis ranks pretty low in the pecking order. Liv's regular crew of followers, including Amber and Meredith, all made a great show of nestling firmly down into their seats, as did every guy who still dreamed of going out with Liv. I was amazed at how many were supporting Jane, though. It looked like almost half the class. God, maybe even more than half.

I was so busy making note of who did and who didn't that I didn't even look at Liv until I heard her gasp softly. I turned in the direction she was looking. Across the room by the window, Alec Burke had gotten to his feet in support of Jane, and was fixing Liv with a look of scathing contempt.

Chapter 16

"It had to have been some kind of joke, right?" Liv asked for the third time.

"Liv, I told you I don't know. I just don't know!" I said, frantic over the furious scowl she was leveling at me.

I had actually been thinking about saying something to Liv, about maybe having crossed the line. But that had all gone out the window when Liv's chances of getting Alec were ruined—and apparently it was all somehow my fault.

"Well you better figure it out fast, Jenna," Liv snapped. "You set me up in this whole thing. You told me Alec was on our side. And I believed you!"

"That's not . . ." My voice faltered. "I mean, I didn't . . ."

I had started to say that it was Liv who had been so

certain Alec was against the dissection ban. But now I wasn't so sure. I couldn't remember how it had unfolded, or what I'd even said.

We were standing in front of the school under the overhang, waiting for the bus. Usually it was easier just to walk home, but today was cold and drizzly.

"This is a complete nightmare," Liv muttered, shaking her head. "You've killed me, Jen. You've totally killed me."

"What the hell was that all about?"

Neither of us had seen Alec approaching. He stood directly in front of us, his wet hair dripping down into his face.

"You said you were on our side," he said to Liv angrily. "And then you pull a stunt like that. I had no idea you were such a bitch, Liv. Did you think what you did was funny?"

"It was all planned, Alec," I said quickly, and I felt Liv stiffen beside me. "She was trying to like, you know, drum up sympathy for Jane. She figured if she made the people who wanted to do the dissection look bad, it would help Jane's chances."

There was a pause as Alec stared at me. Liv seemed to be holding her breath.

"Do I look brain-dead?" Alec finally said. "Give me a break, Jenna. You're as bad as she is." He turned his attention to Liv.

"Just leave her alone, understand? You don't have to agree with her, and you don't have to like her. But leave Jane Walsh alone."

"Sorry, Alec, only dogs like Jane follow orders," Liv said sharply. Alec made a noise of disgust, and walked off without another word.

Liv looked like a different person, standing there with rage coming off her in waves. I *had* to make this better.

"God, I'm sorry, Liv," I said. "I thought I was helping."

"You thought wrong," she snapped.

"People look up to you, Liv," I said. "Maybe if you talked to people and got them to support Jane, Alec would–"

"Don't you dare finish that sentence," Liv interrupted. "You think I would actually stoop so low as to be nice to that . . . thing?"

"I'm sorry," I mumbled.

"You got that right," she said. "And Alec just showed me his true colors too. I wouldn't go out with that loser now if he was the last guy in the world."

"Maybe it's for the best, then–" I began.

"Stop," she interrupted, holding her hand out like a traffic cop. "I need to get away from you for a while, Jen. I can't even look at you."

My eyes filled with tears, and I grabbed her sleeve as she started to go.

"Don't–" I faltered. "Liv, please don't be in a fight with me now. I couldn't take it."

She rolled her eyes, and tried to free her sleeve from my hand.

"I think he's moving out!" I cried. "I think they're splitting up, Liv. He's gonna leave."

There. It was out. I waited for Liv's reaction.

"Oh God," Liv said, sounding more irritated than sympathetic. But she stood her ground, looking in the other direction as the tears ran down my face. Ahead of us, the bus finally pulled up.

Liv hoisted her backpack onto her shoulder.

"You can come to my house," she said, and I almost reeled with relief. "We'll talk.

"But . . ." she continued quickly. "You better help me get back at her, Jen. You're going to help me come up with a plan. Jane will pay for this."

I followed her onto the bus, wondering what that "payment" might be.

Chapter 17

"So I don't know what we're going to end up doing," I was saying. "It's been almost a week, and we haven't come up with anything. I'm just telling you this, you know, because you seemed more interested in it than *Reader's Digest*."

Miss Caples examined the arm of her chair.

"As far as everyone else goes, though, it's been okay," I continued. "Meredith and Amber and those guys were totally on Liv's side anyway. And even the geeks thought it was kind of funny. Biology is a fairly lethal class, after all. And the thing is, you pretty much can't be mad at Liv. I mean, you should see this girl, Miss Caples. She's like . . . you know. What's the name . . . that chick coming out of the big clamshell in the painting, or . . . You know who I mean?"

Miss Caples was attacking the lint collection on her armchair, removing individual pieces with serious purpose.

"Adonis!" I cried. "Oh, no, that's a guy. But you know what I'm saying, right? Everyone wants to be around Liv. It's like you get some of her glow just by being near her, I guess.

"Not that I'm that glow-needy," I added with a grin. "But sometimes when Liv and I are out together, or she's decided just the two of us are going to share a table in the cafeteria, I kind of feel like I'm with a celebrity. People look at us. They're actually jealous. Stuff like that."

She flashed me a skeptical look that was over almost before it began.

I got up then, and crossed over to a large photograph hanging on the wall. It was one I'd never really examined before.

"Is that a cave?"

There was a path, strewn with branches and logs, leading sharply up a hill. The stone face of the hill was marked by a mouth-shaped gap. Through the gap was darkness. A group of five men and women, wearing the same old-style clothes I saw in most of Miss Caples's pictures, were standing in front of what had to be the entrance to a big cave.

"That's her again!" I said, suddenly recognizing the familiar beautiful face. "But she's not wearing that uniform. What an awesome cave. Are they going in, or coming out, I wonder?"

I heard a little chuckle then, just a whisper of a laugh. God knows what she thought was so funny, but the fact of the laugh made me happy. I have to say I'd grown almost comfortable in Miss Caples's company. I got the idea too that she sort of liked listening to me blather on about school, and Alec, and Liv. I only had a couple of looks and a sort of giggle to go on. But I just knew that she didn't mind my company. That she looked forward to it. Her silence now seemed almost a statement. And everything she didn't say sort of intensified her listening, if that makes any sense. I know when Liv's talking to me, I spend a lot of time just thinking of what I'm going to say as soon as there's a break. Miss Caples listens with every molecule in her body. I turned and looked at her, something I was doing a bit more now. She was actually watching my face, and as I looked at her, she raised an eyebrow, indicating that I should go on.

"The thing is, Miss C, my dad moved out on Monday. To a hotel, or something. I have to say, I still can't believe it. I mean, I pretty much told you what's been going on for the last few years and everything. But somehow I never actually thought he'd leave, you know? That's why it's so important I smooth things over with Liv. I know she's kind of changing. Maybe it's the money thing with her dad, maybe she's worried and acting out, or something. If only she'd let me help her. But she won't even talk to me about it. She's always been there for me, and she's there for me now, even when she'd maybe rather not be. And when we're dealing with stuff like that, she's like the old Liv, you know? The way it used to be. God, I couldn't live without that. I'd go totally ape-wad."

I thought about that for a moment, then turned back to the picture of the cave on the wall.

"Who took all these pictures, anyway? This place looks amazing," I said. "Where is it? I haven't traveled that much, so I guess I wouldn't recognize anything. Who are the two guys?"

I squinted and leaned closer, almost pressing my nose against the glass.

"Hey! One of them is really cute."

Really cute was an understatement. The guy was gorgeous.

"She's looking at him," I said, noticing the sidelong glance the beautiful woman was casting. "The guy. He's a poem, Miss Caples, I swear!"

Something made me turn around quickly then. It was almost like a sudden change in the weather, as if a wave of electricity had rolled over the room. She was standing up. Somehow I thought she just stayed in that chair after I left, sitting out the week, until I came back again. But there she was now actually standing, and I felt frozen in place.

And suddenly, as if it were the most natural thing in the world, Miss Caples opened her mouth, and began to speak.

Chapter 18

"Her name is Hannah," she said, walking stiffly past me into the kitchen. "The one on the end is me."

That was all she offered, and for a moment I wondered whether to just let well enough alone. My curiosity won out.

"Where is this place?"

"Mammoth Cave, Kentucky," came her voice from the kitchen, over the sound of running water. She didn't even need to see the picture, I thought.

"Mammoth Cave," I repeated. "Sounds big."

Miss Caples shuffled back into the living room holding a glass of water. She turned to look at me as she passed, and nodded in acknowledgment of my comment. This was as physically close as I'd ever been to her. I noticed for the first time the amazing color of her eyes. They were a light, almost icy blue. The effect was intense. They made her whole face come alive.

"And *that's* you?" I said, examining the picture with amazement. I now recognized her as the friend of the beautiful woman who appeared in so many of the photos.

"1935," she said, settling carefully into her chair.

1935. Almost seventy years ago. Virtually an entire lifetime. I resisted the urge to ask Miss Caples her age. She might have been eighteen or so in the picture. It was weird to think that someone who was practically an adult in 1935 could be sitting in the room with me now.

Miss Caples didn't say anything for several moments. I was afraid of losing the momentum.

"Are you from Kentucky?" I asked. She shook her head.

"A holiday," she said. "After Julian got the motor car."

"Which one is Julian?" I asked.

There was a pause. A small smile played about Miss Caples's mouth.

"The poem," she said.

"Julian," I repeated, looking at him. "Smokin' name. That's a compliment," I added quickly.

"And who's Hannah?" I asked.

"Hannah," Miss Caples said, a little dreamily. "Never was there a truer Venus."

"Venus!" I cried. "That's the one. The chick in the clamshell."

"It was a scallop shell," she replied, a little sternly.

It should have seemed bizarre. Miss Caples hadn't

spoken a word in weeks, and now here she was, chatting, though in relatively short sentences. But somehow it wasn't that weird. And I was practically dying of curiosity.

"But who *was* she?" I pressed.

"She was my best friend. Actually, she was more than a friend. I was entirely devoted to her. Consumed."

She looked miles away. Decades away, maybe would be more accurate.

"What was she like?" I pressed.

Miss Caples fixed her blue eyes on mine.

"Powerful. Breathtaking. Irresistible." She took a breath, and added a final adjective.

"Dangerous."

Chapter **19** *Elspeth*

But not always dangerous. Not in the beginning. There was no place for danger in St. Mary's, between lessons, prayers, chores, and confession. And perhaps danger isn't that simple. Or maybe it is too easy a word. Hannah's danger was like a flash flood that rose over us and carried everyone away before we even knew what was happening. Maybe we could have resisted. Maybe she could have. Or maybe the current was too strong. I just don't know.

Look at us, Jenna of Fire Hill School. Look at us there, seventy years past, framed by the mouth of that black cave. The events unfolding there are rewritten for every generation. I can spell it out if I have to, word for word.

Don't you recognize it? Don't you see the symbols, recognize the pattern?

Chapter **20**

"Aren't you going to say anything?" I asked.

My mother smoothed the curtain back into place and turned from the window.

"I'm sorry," she said weakly. "I know this is happening to both of us. I haven't even asked you how you feel about it, Jen."

I picked up my fork, then put it down again nervously.

"Why don't you sit down and eat something with me," I said. "Hot food. I made it myself."

She pulled up a chair and sat across from me. Even with the circles under her reddened eyes and stray strands of hair bobbing in her face, she still looked so softly pretty. I wondered if she knew that.

"I'm not hungry, sweetheart," she said. "But I'll sit with you and have some soda."

She poured herself a Diet Coke and plopped both of her elbows on the table.

"How are you, Jen?" she asked. I shrugged.

"I don't know," I said honestly. "I feel a lot of different ways. I mean, I'm furious at him and everything. I am. I've had this kind of sick feeling in my stomach since he left. But at the same time, and I don't want you to take this the wrong way, I'm sort of relieved."

She nodded a bit.

"You know, it just seemed like it was a lost cause. Ever since . . . well, for the last couple of years, it's just seemed like we were all stuck in the same sucky place. I would have given anything for things to get better. But lately, I started feeling like that just wasn't going to happen. Now that he's not here, at least maybe you and I can get out of this rut we've been in."

I saw her eyes fill with tears, but she nodded again.

"And Liv's been great," I added. "So that's been kind of a saving grace for me."

It sounded true.

My mother drained her Diet Coke, and poured herself another glass.

"I'm not proud of the way I've behaved, Jen," she said.

"What do you mean?" I asked. "He's the one who behaved badly."

"But I've been weak," she said, looking directly at

me. "I've been playing the victim, wringing my hands. Not allowing myself to be angry. I thought I was stronger than that. I *will* be stronger from now on. It's time I got my life back, and started participating in yours too."

There were still tears in her eyes, but there was also a look of real determination. I felt an overwhelming sense of relief. It was true that since my father's first affair, my mother had kind of disappeared and been replaced by this weepy, silent woman. I was glad she knew it.

"How is your Wednesday afternoon project going?" she asked.

"Well," I said, rolling my eyes, "after like a month of total silence, Miss Caples started talking to me. Like there was nothing strange about it. All this time I thought she totally hated me. Now I'm thinking maybe she was just waiting to get to know me."

"It sounds like perhaps you've gained her trust," my mother said.

"I guess," I said. "I've been looking at her old photographs a lot. They really are cool. I wasn't faking being interested, or anything. And she just started telling me who the people are in them."

"Jenna, that's wonderful," she said, giving me a big smile. "You're having an effect on this woman. An impact. That's one of the greatest things we can do in this life."

"Well, I wouldn't necessarily say I'm making that much of a difference," I said. "I mean it's not like I got her to go outside, or anything. Supposedly she hasn't gone out in, like, five years."

"Sometimes it seems easier to simply withdraw from the world," she said. "But the easiest way out of any problem is usually not the best choice."

I shifted in my chair uncomfortably.

"What, uh, happened with your frog thing?" she asked, finally.

"Ah, so you have been semi-aware of my little dramas," I said with a grin. "The frogs won. No dissection."

"You don't look too happy about that."

"I'm happy not to have to cut a frog open," I said. "But the girl who started the whole protest thing? Jane Walsh? Liv really hates her. I mean, we both do, sort of. Plus, she kind of caused all these problems between Liv and this guy she really liked. So I guess I'm not happy she got what she wanted."

"Life is never simple, is it?" Mom said, and I nodded my head in agreement.

"Let's do something together, Jen," she said suddenly. "Want to go to the movies Friday night?"

"I've got that Halloween dance thing on Friday," I said. "I promised Liv I'd go with her."

"Liv without a date?" she said.

"Yeah. She was sure Alec would ask her, until the whole thing blew up. So now she's doing the 'Mad at Men' thing and I'm doing the 'Girlfriend Solidarity' thing and going with her. I could go to the movies Saturday, though."

"Saturday's great," she said. "Your pick."

"I'll see if I can find something with no guys in it," I said.

"That," she said, getting up from the table, "would be greatly appreciated."

Chapter **21**

Liv was addressing her group loudly, to be heard over the booming sound of dance music being broadcast throughout the gymnasium.

"Did Ellis Green go blind, or is she under the impression she actually looks good in that combo?" Liv was saying, while making the international *L* sign for "loser" with her thumb and index finger. Amber and Meredith rolled their eyes in perfect synchronization.

"Yeah, there's retro, and then there's bargain basement," Amber said, studying Ellis from a distance.

"That's what you get when you pay under ten dollars for a dress," said Meredith. "If you want to play, you gotta pay."

"Her father is, like, a social worker, or something," said Amber. "He probably makes, like, two dollars a year."

"Someone should start a charity to benefit girls with, like, fatal clothes." Meredith began. Liv whirled to face her, and Meredith actually jumped back as if she'd been struck.

"Do I have to listen to this all night?" Liv cried. "Are you capable of any other conversation?"

"God, keep your hair on, Liv," said Meredith. "I was just making an observation. Um, where's Alec?" she asked, prompting Liv to give her another outraged look.

"Like I'd care," Liv answered sharply.

"Thought you two were hitting it off," Meredith continued, a note of fake innocence in her voice.

"I wouldn't go near Alec Burke if my life depended on it," Liv said. "The guy is the Loserland poster boy."

"Hey, Liv? Want to dance?"

We all turned simultaneously to see who'd asked. Clarke Anthony. Football player, loaded, big man on campus, and generally considered a prime piece of real estate. Clarke's well-publicized breakup with Laurie Rich was all over school. Liv's hair seemed to magically fall into place.

"Whatever," she said, but she stood up and looked pretty pleased.

"She'll land him, of course," said Amber wistfully, watching them walk onto the dance floor. "What a stud muffin."

"She can have anyone she wants," I said automatically. I wanted to feel happy for Liv. No matter what she said, I knew she was still feeling the sting of the Alec thing. But I felt somehow strangely removed from Liv's romantic triumphs. And I wasn't experiencing the usual joy I got from witnessing a fashion disaster either. Strangely enough, I found myself thinking about Miss Caples, and wondering what school had been like when she was our age. I made a mental note to ask her about it, now that we were talking.

It seems so unreal. I mean, I can basically picture the cars and clothes and everything, especially after seeing so many of Miss Caples's pictures. But to think of an old person having had a life just like mine, with boys and best friends and disasters in biology class . . . I just can't wrap my mind around it. But sometimes, when I look around at Miss Caples's pictures, or see her eyes come to life as she says the names of her old friends, I can actually begin to believe that life somehow existed before I came along.

"Oh, my God, will you look at that!" Meredith was saying as I suddenly became aware of my surroundings again.

"Where?" I asked, but Amber was already pointing. I looked, and blinked with surprise.

"That's got to be a charity date," Meredith said.

"Or a practical joke," Amber added.

Whatever the reason, Alec Burke and Jane Walsh were dancing up a storm, and looking for all the world like they were having a blast.

I immediately looked for Liv. As soon as I caught sight of her, it was obvious she'd seen them. She was smiling at Clarke, flipping her hair around, but I could tell the joy had gone right out of her.

"I swear, that frog girl gets all of her clothes at Hippies 'R' Us," said Amber.

"It's too boring to even discuss," said Meredith. "Let's reposition by the refreshment table."

Amber nodded, and they got up, glancing at me. I waved them away.

"I'm going to hang out here for a while," I said. Amber shrugged. Without Liv, my stock always fell.

There was a momentary lull as the dance tune ended. On a platform at one end of the gym, the disc jockey fumbled for a moment, then played a slow song. I scanned the room for Jane and Alec, just out of curiosity. They were snuggling into each other, barely dancing but still on the floor. Charity dates *never* included slow dances.

I felt Liv approaching before I actually saw her.

"We're out of here," she snapped, and I got quickly to my feet.

"Right," I said. She was already heading for the exit. I caught up just outside the door, in the parking lot.

"Look, there could be a hundred different reasons for it," I said, and she turned and fixed me with an unnaturally wide-eyed look.

"Reasons for what, Jenna?" she said.

"The Alec and Jane thing," I said, but she just stared dumbly at me.

"Their coming to the dance together. There could be a hundred different reasons, Liv. That's all I'm saying."

"Alec and Jane came together? I was dancing with

Clarke Anthony, in case you've forgotten. Who, by the way, is taking me to dinner tomorrow night."

It was sad, somehow, Liv pretending like that. Until recently, however she acted in "public," she'd always been honest with me.

Liv suddenly came to a full stop and whirled to face me.

"Since you brought up that fat freak, though, I've been meaning to talk to you. I've come up with an idea."

"An idea?" I repeated, stupidly thinking that if I could stall her, I might not have to hear it.

"I know you haven't forgotten that we owe her, Jen. You were supposed to be coming up with a plan yourself."

"Right, yeah," I said, looking away, feeling tense. "Nothing's really come to mind."

"Big surprise," she said, then she narrowed her eyes. "But it doesn't matter. I've thought of the perfect thing."

"What is it?" I said, with a growing feeling of foreboding.

"Frogs," she said, her eyes gleaming. "That conscientious cow thinks she deserves a medal for saving the lives of seventeen slimy frogs."

"You're going to give her a medal?" I asked.

"I'm going to give her the frogs," she said.

"Where are you going to get seventeen frogs?" I asked.

"I'm not," she said, "you are. You're going to get

them, kill them, slice their little bellies open, and put every last one of them in her locker. I'll handle the lock."

I was speechless.

"Don't looked so wigged," she said. "I can get Clarke to help you, if you're squeamish. And if you've got to buy them, I'll kick in the cash."

"You can't be serious, Liv," I said.

"Let the punishment fit the crime, isn't that what they say?" Liv asked. "This fits, I'd say. Am I not a genius?"

Maybe she was losing her mind. Actually going crazy. Maybe it was as simple as that.

"I can't do it!" I cried.

Liv gave me a dangerous look that made my stomach lurch. "Oh, and why is that?" she asked.

"For a lot of reasons, Liv. Come on, you have to think of another way."

Liv's expression suddenly shifted. "Haven't I been there for you, Jen, since your dad left? Haven't I sat with you for hours on end, listening to you go on about the whole tacky affair?"

I couldn't do anything but nod. Liv took my hand in her own.

"You know I'd move heaven and earth for you, babe-o-la. All I'm asking you to do is help play a stupid trick on a useless girl. She messed with me, Jen, and I want her to pay for it. One trick, and then it's done. But I need you to help me."

"I don't know what to say, Liv," I said. In the brief silence that followed, I heard the sound of laughter coming from across the parking lot. The bobbing orange points of light I saw there gave away the older cool crowd, sneaking cigarettes. Liv began to walk in their direction without me.

"You *do* know, Jen," she called over her shoulder. "And you *will* do it."

Chapter **22**

Miss Caples just stared at me. She was silent long enough for me to think I might have imagined our conversation last week.

"Anyway," I said, "that's all. Unless you happen to know where I can get seventeen frogs. Cheap. Just kidding. Bet your friend Hannah never asked you to sacrifice amphibians, huh?"

I felt something rub against my ankles, and I bent down to stroke the cat. He gave a contented purr and tried to sit on my feet. When I looked up, Miss Caples had the faraway look in her eyes, an affectionate smile on her face.

"She'd have done it herself," she said, with a little chuckle. "With great glee, I imagine."

"Hannah would?" I asked, and she nodded. "How did you meet her?"

"We were all at St. Mary's," she said. I didn't recognize the name.

"A Catholic girls' school," Miss Caples continued. "Boarding school, you might call it. Really more of a convent school. We all had our reasons for being there. My family was very religious, you see. There weren't many things in life they thought appropriate for a young girl to be doing. They thought sending me to St. Mary's would keep me safe. I met Hannah the first day I arrived."

She gave another chuckle, rocking slightly in her chair with the pleasure of the memory.

"Oh how the Sisters agonized over Hannah. She was like a stunning whirlwind, so breathless and fearless and full of life. And she was the most beautiful girl any of us had ever seen, with an astonishing figure. I remember when we picked up our uniforms, the Sisters gave Hannah one that must have been three times too big. They wanted to hide her. Cover her up," she said, smiling. "But you might as well have tried to cover up the sun."

She paused, and I studied her face, willing her to continue.

"She chose me," Miss Caples said, shaking her head. "Out of everyone there, she chose me to be her friend. I was so overwhelmed with gratitude by that. So overcome. She thrilled me, you see. There wasn't anything Hannah wouldn't do, or say. She was going to travel everywhere and do everything. Be a dancer, a writer, an explorer. And when I was with her, sometimes I felt I could do those things too. She gave me my first camera, showed me how to use it. Said I had a real creative flair. I took most of the pictures in this room with it, which is why I'm not in many of them. Hannah said that I could come along on her dance tours or her exploring expeditions and take photographs. I was so excited to be included in her plans, no matter how far-fetched they sounded. Sometimes I really believed we'd go off to Africa together. Hannah could have done it. I'd always been such a timid child. My whole family was rather reserved. Hannah brought me out of myself, helped me see things in myself I didn't even know were there. It was such a gift."

"She sounds amazing," I said. "Did you stay in touch with her after school?"

"For a time," she replied, her expression of pleasure fading. "Please bring me that photograph," she added, suddenly. I looked up.

"What? Which one?"

She was pointing at the wall across from her armchair.

"The cave one I was looking at last week?"

"Yes," Miss Caples said. "Bring that to me, please."

I pulled the framed picture off of the wall. Behind it was an unfaded, square section of wallpaper the sun probably hadn't hit in decades. I gave the picture a quick dust, and brought it to Miss Caples. She held it in her lap and studied it for a moment.

"I want to tell you something," she said. "Something I haven't spoken about in nearly a lifetime."

"A story?" I asked.

"A story," she said, looking at the picture. "Or a confession. The worst thing I ever did."

At first I thought she might be joking, but her expression was severe, and a little removed. I sat on the rug near her chair, and her cat climbed into my lap. She held the photograph outward for me to see.

"You know where I am in this picture, and you know about Hannah. The man she's looking at is her brother, Julian. The woman standing in between them is Hattie Griggs. She was at St. Mary's with Hannah and me. Hattie wanted to marry Julian, and I think he truly loved her. But Hannah hated Hattie."

"Why?" I asked.

"A hundred reasons. Hattie was what we called a 'charity student.' The school took on one or two girls from poor families every year. Everyone knew who they were. And Hattie was rather awkward, and very shy. She suffered from nerves, as we put it in those days. Sometimes she'd wake us all up, screaming with her nightmares. The darkness made her so fearful, she'd just weep and weep until the sun came up."

"She doesn't sound like all that great a catch," I said, and Miss Caples nodded.

"Oh, but in many ways she was quite special," she said. "There was a pureness about Hattie, an innocence, that was very attractive. She was very sweet. And she had as good a heart as anyone I've ever known. Hattie worked diligently with the troubled and poor. She really had nothing of her own, except Julian. I think all Hattie ever wanted was to be with him and to help people. But sometimes the world just seemed to become too much for her. And the nighttime episodes got worse and worse. We hid it from the nuns at first, thinking that we were protecting her. But of course we were really just making it all worse."

I studied the picture, trying to imagine the mousy, earnest young woman I saw there screaming in the grip of a nightmare. A little shudder ran up my spine, and I looked away from her face.

"Who's the other guy?" I asked, pointing.

"The man whom Hannah would eventually marry," she said. "Their families had known each other for a long time, and both favored the match. Christopher was always around, even when we were at St. Mary's. He'd be waiting out on the street for her after vespers. Some of Hannah's wildest escapades began as ways to avoid him. But they married in the end, as everyone knew they would. This was during the Depression, you see. Hannah's own family actually came through the stock market crash more or less intact, but she was made all too aware of what happened to those in her circle who didn't. Hannah's parents, particularly her father, whom she adored, were determined that Hannah make a suitable match. And in terms of money and social position, Christopher was more than suitable."

"He's not exactly a babe," I said, looking back and forth between his coarse face and Hannah's radiant beauty.

"It didn't matter," Miss Caples said. "He was an important and powerful man."

We sat silently for a moment, then Miss Caples took a deep breath.

"You have to understand how devoted I was to Hannah," she said. "I adored her. Everyone did. I would have followed her to the ends of the earth if she'd asked me. She was like . . . a star. Radiant, celestial. When she came into a room, no one could take their eyes off of her. Men, women. Everyone stared. But at first she thought nothing of it. She'd been beautiful since she was a tiny child. She once told me her earliest memories were of people staring, admiring her, making her the center of their world. Hannah took that attention as her due. And she had an incredible mind. A sharp wit that cut to the bone. Literally fearless. It fueled her antics and her crazy plans and wild ways. But as she got older, I think she grew disillusioned. She realized she couldn't have the life and position in society she wanted and also climb mountains, or dance in a modern troupe, or whatever her plan was that day. And that began to harden her."

"What happened to her?" I asked.

"Hannah gained a more dangerous sense of her power over others. And I think maybe, in a sense, she thought she was just being practical, realistic."

"Practical in what way?" I asked.

"Protecting herself, taking care of the future she could have, even if it wasn't the one she had wanted," Miss Caples replied.

She stared at the photograph in her lap.

"Around the time this photograph was taken, what Hannah wanted most was to drive Hattie Griggs away from our circle—and away from her brother. I don't know if she would have thought any girl was good enough for Julian. As a young man, Julian was given more freedom to choose whom he would marry, but for Hannah, Hattie certainly didn't fit the bill. She couldn't stand to see them together."

"What did she do?" I asked.

Miss Caples looked into my eyes.

"Hannah took every opportunity to needle Hattie. And I was her accomplice. When Julian drove us all to Mammoth Cave for a holiday, Hannah asked me to help her play a little trick on Hattie. It seemed harmless enough, but I should have known better. Actually, I did know better, but I didn't care. The light in Hannah's eyes when she told me the plan was all I needed."

The cat came suddenly awake, and leaped out of my lap.

"There is a famous story connected to Mammoth Cave," Miss Caples continued. "You probably aren't aware of it."

I shook my head.

"A boy named Floyd Collins went exploring the caves sometime in the twenties. He went very far underground, exploring the tunnels, and as he was crawling through a narrow one, he slipped and got stuck. His family came looking for him and heard him calling out. But they weren't able to free him, so one of them sent for help.

"Although the rescue people could almost get to him, they couldn't pull him free either. Days passed, over a week. There were a thousand people gathered there—people trying to help, people who had come to watch, newspaper reporters. You'd see a picture in the paper of a man preaching and waving a Bible at the crowd, and ten feet away another man would be selling hot dogs. I remember listening with my parents to radio news up-dates being broadcast live from the scene. We would all pray for him, and each day they didn't rescue him, I thought I hadn't prayed hard enough. They were able to get the boy food, and water, but he was stuck fast. No one could help. Finally, the ground gave way and caved in. By the time they finally got to him, he was dead."

"That's awful," I whispered, and she nodded.

"It surely was, poor child. Little Floyd Collins. No one could talk about anything else, for ages. Wedged twenty feet underground, encased in rock, unable to move an inch. Begging for a doctor to cut his legs off and free him. Trapped for almost two weeks before finally dying. We all had nightmares about it for months."

I had a feeling I might be having a nightmare or two myself about poor Floyd Collins.

"Anyway," she went on, "by the time we visited Mammoth Cave, it had been some years since the Collins boy had died. Hannah had picked the spot. Her aunt and uncle lived quite nearby and arranged for us to stay with them, so it was all very proper. But you can be sure the Collins story was something that we all thought about, to one degree or another. Hannah always seemed to joke and make light of it, but Hattie was pretty spooked. I hadn't really made the connection yet, you see, that Hattie's worst nerve attacks tended to come at night, when it was dark. It just never occurred to me to consider what a cave might represent for her. And I was pretty frightened of that cave myself, for that matter. But Hannah wanted to go exploring, so we all agreed. And that's when Hannah came up with the idea."

"The . . . idea," I repeated hesitantly. Miss Caples nodded.

"It was meticulously thought out. The five of us were walking through some of the caverns. The men both had lanterns, and Hannah and I had our own small candles. We had a roll of twine, and we unwound it as we walked, leaving a trail of string behind us so that we could find our way out. Hannah pretended to twist her ankle, and she asked Julian and Christopher to help her out of the cave. I asked Hattie if she wouldn't mind continuing with me for just a little while, as if I wasn't yet ready to leave. I knew she didn't want to stay in that cave. But Julian was already helping Hannah out, assuring us over his shoulder that he'd be back in a few minutes. Hattie was self-conscious about her little nerve episodes, and I'm sure she didn't want Julian to see how frightened she was. So she agreed rather nervously to stay with me, and after we had descended a good way into one of the tunnels, I told her I could hear someone shouting something down to us. I had the twine, and I asked her to just wait a moment, so I could go around the bend for a minute to better hear what they were saying. But that's not what I did. Instead, I hurried up and out of the cave, pulling all the twine with me, and I left Hattie there, in complete darkness, all alone."

Miss Caples paused, and brushed a strand of hair from her face with a shaking hand.

"Hannah was bent double with laughter when I got out of the cave. Julian quickly got the truth out of her, and he grabbed one of the lanterns and ran back into the cave after Hattie. But I'd pulled up all the twine, and he couldn't remember which way we'd gone down. There were so many different tunnels, so many passageways and dead ends ... At first when she heard the sound of Julian's voice, Hattie called to him over and over. But the sound just bounced off all the walls, and the echo kept drawing Julian in the wrong direction. Finally, she stopped calling altogether."

"She died?" I asked, stunned.

"No," Miss Caples said, shaking her head. "But by the time Julian brought her out, she was ... she'd had a kind of breakdown. It had taken him hours to get to her. She was ... it was too much for her, sitting there in the cold and the blackness with God knows what skittering around her. Those fears that had been slipping into her dreams back at St. Mary's must have absolutely overcome her in that cave. There she was with no friends to comfort her—no sun on its way up. She literally went out of her mind with fright. She was never the same."

"I guess I can see why," I said weakly.

"We all went back to school as if it had never happened, but by then it was obvious even to the nuns that something was seriously wrong with Hattie. In just a short span of time she withdrew into herself entirely. No one could reach her. Finally, she was taken out of school and put into a kind of institution. And I could have prevented it from getting out of control from the beginning by telling the Sisters what was happening to her in the night—that she needed help. And I *should* have realized what a dangerous game it was taking her into that cave. But I didn't. Instead, I ruined Hattie's future. The life she could have had with Julian. All for the love of Hannah."

Those cornflower blue eyes fixed intently on mine.

"So tell me, Jenna of Fire Hill School. How do you feel about those frogs now?"

Chapter 23

I took a long walk alone, the kind I used to take with Liv, on our road. There is never much traffic there, and the delicious smell of fall, and the crunching of brown and yellow leaves under my feet, helped calm me and clear my mind. I passed the old cemetery, and was now doubling back toward home.

I had thought about Miss Caples and Hannah, and poor Hattie and even Floyd Collins almost constantly since she'd told me the story. Although I didn't think it was too likely that Jane would lose her marbles over a few dead frogs, I could imagine how much it would upset her.

Miss Caples must have recognized from the beginning that my friendship with Liv was something of a reflection of hers and Hannah's. My mother has always said there's no such thing as a coincidence–that everything happens for a reason. I believed that too. So I took Miss Caples's warning, and it definitely was a warning, very seriously. I could see that she wanted me to think about the consequences of messing with another person. After all, I didn't know Jane all that well anymore, but she seemed pretty sensitive, the heart-on-her-sleeve type. Was I really the kind of person who could hurt someone that way, let alone find it funny? And if the answer was no, as I knew it was, then why on earth do it?

The answer, of course, was Liv. So far, I hadn't lost her. She was still mine to run to, to brandish like a prize. Yes, in a way, Liv was a trophy friend. But our history went deeper than that. She was my best friend, the only one who truly knew me inside and out. But if I refused to do what Liv wanted, would she continue to be my friend?

Two years ago I would have said yes, without question. Two years ago a team of wild horses couldn't have dragged the two of us apart. But something had changed. Maybe if her family problems hadn't occurred, this might not have happened to us. But they had. And somehow, I knew that her family was really only part of it.

I could see my house now, ablaze with light against the darkening November sky. There were signs of movement through the kitchen window. So far my mother had been as good as her word. She was getting out more, finding constructive ways to express her anger at my father, and helping me do the same. Maybe the most significant clue that I was getting the old mom back was her cooking. Almost every night, she was making these amazing dishes, lingering at the table with me long after we'd finished every bite. At that thought, I felt a hollow growling in my stomach, and picked up the pace.

Across the street, Mrs. Madison's house was bleakly unlit. I paused long enough to look at it for a few moments. If Miss Caples had been young once, and full of the future, then so certainly had Mrs. Madison. What had the twenty-year-old Mrs. Madison been like? Who had she cared about? Could she have had any inkling of the miserable old lady she would someday become?

And more importantly, if she had known, would she have changed a thing?

Chapter **24**

I told Liv my decision that morning while we were waiting for the bus. She was standing less than a foot away. I know she heard me. But a silent stare was her only comment. When the bus finally came, and we got in, I understood without being told that we'd be sitting in separate seats.

By the end of first period, as I filed into the hallway, it became obvious where things stood.

"Hey, Mer," I said automatically as I made my way to my locker. "Howdy, Amber."

I had gotten my combination lock opened and had my hand on my locker when I became aware of the overwhelming silence that had followed my greetings. Suddenly motionless, I gave what I hoped was a casual glance in their direction.

Meredith and Amber were standing shoulder to shoulder, staring at me. Amber had a triumphant smile on her face. Meredith had affected an I'm-*so*-not-talking-to-you sneer. When they saw me turn to look at them, Amber made a little gun out of her thumb and forefinger. She pointed it at me, and pretended to pull the trigger. As she blew on her finger, Meredith made a sound halfway between a giggle and a shriek.

Whatever. I should hardly have expected any less from Liv's mindless slave twins. I heard a locker open to my left, and turned to see Jessica Davies, our class vice president. Jess and I had never been particularly close, but we'd never been on bad terms either.

"Hey," I said with a grin, grateful for the opportunity to make some conversation. "Study for the English quiz?"

She just tossed a few books into her locker and retrieved a sweater. I repeated the question.

"So, did you study for the quiz?"

Jess slammed her locker closed, spun the lock, and turned to face me. She stood regarding me with detachment as she slipped one, then the other arm into her sweater. Then, slinging her backpack over her shoulder, she walked past me and down the hall.

The whole situation seemed suddenly dreamlike and unreal. Another five minutes in the hallway confirmed that almost half the class had stopped talking to me. I had never been treated this way in my life.

It was stupid of me to think things might be less difficult at lunch. I sat by myself at an out-of-the-way table by the fire exit, hoping just to be left alone. Unfortunately, my chosen position gave practically the entire lunchroom an unobstructed view of me. I tried to block out the gesturing in my direction, and the snickering, but my efforts were pretty futile.

At a table near the salad bar, Ellis Green had gotten to her feet and was marching toward me with great purpose, throwing the occasional glance over at Liv's table to make sure she was being observed. That really irritated me, because Ellis had made a career out of getting dumped on by Liv. I guess she just couldn't pass up the opportunity to gloat at my downfall. That, and maybe she was hoping to score some points with Liv.

When Ellis reached my table, she didn't say anything. She simply reached over the table, picked up my carton of milk, and poured its contents over my head.

The room erupted with laughter, and I felt like I was drowning in the milk that had seeped into my ears and mouth. I wiped my face furiously, picking individual voices out of the roar. Payback is a bitch, I heard someone say. And so is she, another added. But it was Liv's voice that reached me the most directly.

"Ellis!" she cried, helpless with laughter. "That was priceless, babe-o-la!"

Hearing *my* nickname directed at the loathsome Ellis pushed me over the top. The noises and faces became a blur as I ran from the cafeteria to the girls' room. Once inside, I stuck my head under the faucet and washed as much of the milk from my hair as I could. I caught sight of my reflection in the mirror. My red hair dripped as I rubbed brown paper towels over it. My face was a burning crimson, with glassily matching eyes. I relaxed my hand and let the paper towels drop to the floor as the sobs overtook me. They were the huge, breath-robbing kind, and I didn't try to stop them.

When my sobs finally began to weaken, I splashed cold water over my face and looked at myself in the mirror. By this time I was a study in red: hair, eyes, nose, cheeks. All variations of brick to crimson. I shook my head with disgust, then jumped slightly at the sound of a toilet flushing. The stall door opened, and still looking in the mirror, I watched the occupant emerge.

"Well, what do you know," said the last person in the world that I wanted to see. "Welcome to the club, Jenna."

Jane Walsh joined me at the sink, and peered around to look into my swollen eyes.

"So," she said with a small smile. "What are you in for?"

Chapter **25**

If Miss Caples was surprised to see me, unannounced and on a Friday, she hid it pretty well.

"So anyway," I said, "I just thought you'd want to know what I told her, and everything. So you wouldn't be in suspense."

She nodded seriously.

"Well," I said, beginning to feel stupid, "I guess I should go, then."

"I admire you," she said suddenly.

"You admire me?" I asked, and she nodded.

"Look how easy it was for you," she said. "You did it, and it's done."

"Easy?" I cried. "Look at me, Miss Caples. Don't you think there's a reason my face looks like a catcher's mitt?

The whole school is laughing at me. No one will speak to me.

"Except Jane Walsh." I gave a little laugh. "Jane is the only person in school who said two civil words to me today. She actually welcomed me to the club. The newest loser has officially arrived."

"You have a strength that will sustain you throughout your life," Miss Caples said sadly. "If I had one ounce of what you possess, Hattie Griggs might have had a normal life. In the real world, with Julian. And I might not be hiding in this apartment. It will never get any worse than this, Jenna, and in the end, you will have peace because you did the right thing. I long for peace. I shall never have it."

"Why . . ." I began, then faltered. Although I felt very close to Miss Caples now, I still wondered if there were some subjects I should leave alone.

"Ask the question," she said tonelessly.

"I just was going to ask . . . I mean, why don't you go outside? Why did you stop?"

She nodded as if she'd been expecting the question.

"It's something that happened by degrees," she said. "First I stopped going out in the evenings. I'd just come straight home from my job at the bank. When I retired from work, I stopped going out completely, except to get groceries. Then they began a delivery service, and that put an end to my shopping trips. When I quit going to church, that was really the end. It was so important to me, the quiet and the music and the worship. It reminded me of those first months with Hannah, at St. Mary's. But nothing I had deprived myself of seemed enough of a punishment, so I took church away too. I don't know when the last time was that I went out. There was no decision that it would be my final trip. One day I just realized it had been weeks, a month. Five years."

"But there's nothing stopping you, right?" I asked. "I mean, you could just open the door and walk to the sidewalk and back, couldn't you?"

She shook her head almost fiercely.

"No, not at all," she said very softly. "That would be quite impossible."

"I don't understand," I said, frustrated. "I mean, why?"

"Too much time has passed, Jenna," she said. "Hiding has become a way of life for me—hiding from my fears, from what I've done, and now hiding from the world. I'm not sure you even breathe the same air I once did."

"What about your friends? Don't you want to see them?"

Miss Caples gave a short, sharp laugh.

"Even if I looked for the few friends I once had, I wouldn't find them. Don't think it's a bed of roses living this long. Most everybody leaves you behind sooner or later."

"I won't do that," I said. "And I'm your friend, aren't I?"

The dark expression on Miss Caples's face had been overwritten by a glimpse of pleasure. I felt my own sense of power at that moment. It felt really good.

"And anyway, you don't know for certain who's dead and gone. What about Hattie? Didn't you ever hear any news about her, Miss C?" I asked. "About what happened to her later on in life?"

"Oh yes," said Miss Caples. "The institution she was placed in is just outside Fire Hill. WindHill, it's called. She finally died there, some time in the late sixties. They closed her account at the bank that year, you see, and I saw the paperwork. It had the word 'deceased' stamped across it in red ink. I didn't go to the funeral."

"Didn't you ever try to get in touch with Hattie before she died? Or Hannah?" I asked. "With all of you living so close to each other, and everything?"

Miss Caples shook her head.

"I couldn't," she said. "No, that isn't true. I just wouldn't."

"Why not?" I asked.

"I was so, so ashamed at what I'd done," she said. "I had no backbone, no courage. So instead, I hid, especially from Hattie. I just wasn't worthy of her. I often wish I knew exactly how she died, and whether anyone was with her. Where she's buried—what her headstone looks like. It would help, somehow, to know. I'd like to light a candle in her memory. I suppose she was quite alone by the end. And it was all my doing," she said.

"You know, I've been thinking about that," I said, sitting heavily in a chair. "You don't know that you're responsible for Hattie going . . . well, having to go to the institution. I mean yes, you probably made it happen at that particular time. But you said yourself she had those nighttime episodes as long as you knew her. It sounds to me like she was going to snap sooner or later. You just maybe made it happen sooner, that's all."

She stared at the wall.

"And if she never got out," I continued, "if she never got better, she obviously had a serious problem. That cave thing was just one factor, Miss Caples."

"It wasn't just the cave," Miss Caples said, looking weary.

"What do you mean?" I asked.

"There was more," she said. "After. When Hattie was in WindHill."

I waited. Miss Caples looked as if she was gathering her strength, somehow, getting ready to tell me. Her expression seemed to turn inward.

"Julian wrote her letters," she said, finally. "He'd had an accident, broken his leg very badly and sustained other serious injuries as well. After he was released from the hospital, he went to his parents' house to convalesce. Hannah was still living at home, it was another year or two before she and Christopher were married. Hannah immediately took over Julian's care—wanted to do everything for him herself. The family certainly could have afforded a professional nurse, but Hannah refused. Her parents gave in to her after a while, and then left on one of their interminable holidays. Hannah asked me to stay with her. Naturally I came straightaway without question. Julian was quite incapacitated for several months, you see. And WindHill didn't allow patients to receive phone calls, except from immediate family. But Julian wrote to Hattie regularly during this time. He wanted her to know that he intended to wait for her, that he still loved her, and wouldn't abandon her. And that he'd come to see her as soon as he could."

"How do you know all that?" I asked.

"He told me," she said. "Julian was as dazzled by his sister as the rest of us, and Hannah claimed she never meant any harm, but by then I think Julian didn't quite trust her as far as Hattie was concerned. And the reason I know that is because Julian didn't give Hannah his letters to mail. He gave them to me."

She stopped for a long time, and looked off into the distance.

"You see, after the cave incident, I had gone to Julian and told him how sorry I was about what had happened to Hattie. He forgave me by trusting me–those letters were a second chance to make things right. Julian never specifically asked me not to tell Hannah," she continued. "But I knew that was his intention. And I told her anyway."

"You did?" I asked, slightly shocked.

"Yes, I did," she said. "And each week I took those letters from Julian, along with his grateful thanks, and I delivered them into Hannah's hands. Hattie never received a single one of them."

"So Hattie never knew that Julian was waiting for her?" I asked.

"Never," Miss Caples said. "If the people at the institution had known, it *might* have made a difference. You see, there was no one who would step forward and take responsibility for Hattie. Her parents were alive, but they were poor and elderly, and didn't even understand the kind of help she needed. But Julian would have looked after her. He had plenty of money. And he loved her. But as month after month went by, without any response from Hattie, I guess Julian's confidence in their love began to weaken. And that's when Hannah seized the opportunity. Hattie's silence, Hannah told him, confirmed her wish to be left alone. If he really cared about her, he should respect that decision. Hannah kept at him week after week, and finally Julian began to believe it. Eventually, he stopped writing and planning to visit her altogether.

"So, you see," she said, finally making eye contact with me, "it was so much more than a trick gone wrong. And I hated myself for what I'd done—even more than I loved Hannah. That was when I destroyed our friendship. I literally forced her to drive me away. By the time she and Christopher set a wedding date, I didn't expect an invitation. She didn't even contact me when Julian was killed, earlier in the year."

"He was killed?" I cried, thinking of his lean, handsome young face.

"Everyone was devastated," Miss Caples said softly. "Though Hannah wasn't speaking to me, I heard the news from others. It was in the Spanish civil war. Like so many passionate young men with strong convictions and, perhaps, not enough to keep them home, Julian couldn't wait to go to Spain and fight against the Facists. He had no business being there, with his leg the way it was. Julian hadn't been in Spain more than a week or two when he was killed."

"That's . . ." I shook my head, at a loss for words.

"After that," she said, "I saw Hannah from time to time, mostly at the bank, but we never spoke. I heard things, though, from other people. Her parents, from all accounts, just fell apart when Julian was killed. They packed up and moved away to somewhere warm, I remember hearing. And after Hannah's wedding, she and Christopher took over the big house. I'd see their names in the society pages every now and then. Perhaps in the beginning she was happy. But I remember Christopher as an emotionless and cold man. No children came along, and when Christopher died suddenly, barely into his thirties, Hannah must have thought, well, she wasn't a dancer or a mountain climber, or even a wife. She was just a widow, all alone in that big house. At least, that's how I always imagined it went."

Miss Caples shook her head with resignation.

"She'd given up all her dreams, you see, for him. She was no longer the Hannah I knew. She was Mrs. Christoper Madison."

Madison?

"Hannah's last name is Madison?" I asked. Miss Caples nodded.

"Miss Caples, do you remember where she lived?"

Miss Caples looked at me as if she thought I was a little stupid.

"Of course I remember," she said. "I haven't lost my mind—not yet, anyway. Who could forget that massive old house? She always was so proud of it. Swore she'd never leave it until the day she died."

She paused, and I squirmed with impatience.

"So where is it?" I asked.

She got that slightly distant look on her face that I was beginning to recognize.

"Orchard Road," she said.

Orchard Road. My road. Miss Caples's Hannah was my Mrs. Madison.

Chapter **26** *Elspeth*

The years have made me even more naive. To think I honestly believed I would receive some kind of absolution for my confession. Seventy years and never told a soul. I could tell the world today, and it wouldn't matter. They're long dead and gone . . . Julian . . . Hattie. I must be done with it, then. There will be no inner peace for me, and I must accept that for every year Hattie lived without Julian, for every precious month Julian had left that he lived without Hattie, I will pay my penance.

But why, suddenly, is it not enough? I've lived with it for seventy years. Why, now, is it eating through my heart? Why am I so desperate to fix what has lain sleeping for nearly a lifetime?

I helped Jenna prevent someone else from getting hurt. I believe she now understands the danger of the power her friend wields. This should suffice. A small action taken, on behalf of someone Hattie and Julian never knew . . . but a step nonethe-less. But I realize now that instead of closure, I have flung the door wide open. One way or the other, I must walk through.

But how? What can I do for them now, except to hunt down their graves and clear away the weeds? Even in so doing, per-haps I would only bring them more dishonor by my presence. I am too frightened to find their graves, too frightened to kneel by them. I do not know what to do. And I am too afraid.

Though I do not feel I can go ahead, I know neither can I go back. I am so tired. . . .

Chapter 27

"Mom? Can you hear me?"

Her car was in the driveway, and her purse was on the kitchen table, but she wasn't responding.

Things had changed around our house. Mom was now keeping much closer tabs on me. I should have thought to let her know my plans, or at least called her from Miss Caples's apartment. Had she gotten worried and gone out on foot looking for me? Or worse, had she called Liv's?

I heard a noise from the direction of the living room. Before I could investigate, my mother walked into the hallway, the cordless phone pressed to her ear. She nodded at me and raised her index finger in the "hang on" sign. Her face looked grim.

"Yes, that's right," she was saying. "Madison. I'm her neighbor."

It took everything I had not to interrupt.

"I understand. And you have my number? Good, I appreciate it. Thank you."

"Mom?" I asked. "What's going on?"

"Oh honey," she said, putting a hand on my shoulder. "It's Mrs. Madison. She's had a stroke."

Mrs. Madison. Hannah. I could hardly bring myself to think of them as one and the same person. I'd been so shocked by the realization, I hadn't even told Miss Caples I lived across the street from her. Truth was, I didn't know quite how she'd take it.

It seemed so crazy. How could that young, gorgeous Hannah of the fading black-and-white photographs be the same person as loony, nasty old Mrs. Madison? When had that change happened? When she lost her husband? Or Julian? Or did it go even farther back, to when she lost Miss Caples, and all of their dreams?

"What happened?" I asked. "Is she going to be okay? Is she still . . ."

"It was this morning, just after the bus picked you up," she said. "She called me."

"She *called* you?"

"You know I've always made it clear to Mrs. Madison that I'm here to help, Jen," my mother said, looking surprised.

"No, I know," I said. "It's just that I can't imagine . . . her actually taking you up on it, you know?"

"Well, she'd had a little stroke, and she knew something was very wrong. I went straight over, and called an ambulance. The second stroke happened while I was waiting with her. I hate to think what would have happened if she'd been alone."

"Is it bad?" I asked.

"It's going to take a while before they're certain," she said. "There's a medication they can give you now, right after you've had a stroke, that can combat some of the more devastating permanent effects. But she is a very old lady. I stayed with her at the hospital until about an hour ago. When I left, Mrs. Madison couldn't speak at all, and didn't seem to be able to move her right arm."

"What will happen to her?"

My mother sighed, and began fixing herself a cup of tea.

"Well, hopefully once she's stabilized, she'll be able to come home. She's got a lot of money. I'm sure she could afford to have someone look after her. It makes such a difference, Jen, for a person to be in their own home when they're ill or disabled. You're too young to remember your grandfather, but when he was very sick, Mama brought him home and he lived his last months there. It meant so much to him."

All I could think was that I had to call Miss Caples. I was itching to get to the phone. But suddenly I wondered exactly what it was I would say to her. "Hey, Miss Caples, guess what–your Hannah is my Mrs. Madison–I live across the street from her, but she just had a stroke and can't talk . . ." No. Best to see how things developed before letting Miss Caples know.

"Anyway, I've let the people at the hospital know that I'd like to help out in getting her home. I can't be there all the time, but I can certainly look in on her every day."

"I could help too," I said, totally shocked to hear myself saying it.

"Oh Jen," she said, putting an arm around me. "You're wonderful. You really are, sweetheart."

I returned the hug, enjoying the quiet intimacy of the embrace.

"Listen, honey," my mother said as I gazed around the room. "There is one more thing I need to tell you."

As soon as she said it, my eye fell on the manila-colored envelope on the table.

"I'm not contesting the divorce or anything," she said. "It's what we both want. So by this time next year, more or less . . ."

"What?" I said, already knowing.

"It'll all be over. We'll be officially on our own."

I looked at her for a long time, thinking of her spending her day with Mrs. Madison, and her evening on the phone with the hospital, all while the divorce paperwork sat, already opened, on the table. I felt my love for my mother flare up fiercely.

I took both of her hands in mine.

"Okay then," I said firmly. "All we need is each other, Mom."

Tears spilled out of her eyes as she squeezed my hands, but she smiled through them, and I smiled back. In the yellow light of the kitchen I felt truly happy for the first moment in a very, very long time.

Chapter 28

"Is this seat taken?"

Alec and Jane both stood, with somewhat amused defiance, by my table in the cafeteria.

"Well," I said, surveying the painfully obvious vacancies at the table, "unless a party of twelve shows up, I think I can fit you in."

They both laughed, and sat down across from me.

"So are you guys stapled together, or what?" I asked, not sure if their synchronicity was endearing or irritating.

"Now that's an idea," said Alec, with a grin. Jane glanced at him, and her face flushed scarlet. He really was good looking. I had a fleeting thought of Liv, and did my best to banish her image quickly from my mind. But I couldn't really avoid the actual view I had of her holding court at the other end of the cafeteria.

"It isn't easy, is it?" Jane asked, seeing me watch Liv.

I started to shake my head, then I looked at her, suspicious of the look of sympathy on her face.

"Okay, what are you two up to?" I asked. "You might as well tell me. My life can't get any worse, so I wouldn't waste any energy plotting against me."

"Plotting against you?" said Alec, half laughing. "You think we're plotting against you?"

"I'm afraid it's nothing as exciting as that, Jenna," said Jane. "We need to eat. You need to eat. And I know it's no fun sitting by yourself, particularly with that audience cheering you on."

I shook my head.

"I don't get it," I said.

"How's that?" asked Alec softly.

"You know," I said, but they both just looked at me. I sighed.

"All right. I was mean to you, Jane. I've never been exactly nice to you, but lately I've been really nasty. And I've supported Liv in her . . . efforts along the same lines."

Jane nodded, gazing at me evenly. I noticed for the first time that her eyes were an amazing shade of blue. She had long eyelashes too. The kind you can't fake.

"So . . ." I continued. "Now Liv has dumped me, and taken most of the school with her. And you're suddenly taking it upon yourself to sit with me at lunch? What gives?"

Jane continued to look calmly at me, a small smile playing about her mouth. I'd never really examined her face before, but now I seemed to see a lack of . . . decep-tiveness? That was it. When I looked at Jane, I felt I could take her at face value.

"Maybe this is kind of *my* way of getting back at *you,*" she said, finally.

I partially raised both my hands to request more of an explanation.

"When things would get really bad at school," she continued, "my mom would tell me that the worst thing I could do to someone being mean to me was to ignore them. Or even be nice back. She said it would totally take the wind out of their sails. I've tried to stick to that."

It was true. In all the time I'd known Jane, I'd never heard her react to being teased. Jane was definitely one of those take-the-high-road types of people.

"The truth is, Jenna, I don't particularly like a fight, at least one on a personal level. I try and save that energy for the things I really believe in. Basically, I just want everyone to be happy. Trouble is," she added with a small smile, "some people haven't felt the same way about me."

"Tiny minds, Jane," said Alec, looking at her with af-fection. A sudden blush of pleased embarrassment crossed Jane's face and she beamed, not quite able to look at him. She might as well have had "He's my first boyfriend!" tattooed across her forehead. Then she seemed to remember herself, suddenly, and gave me a serious look.

"If all this had to happen for us to be friends, Jen, that's fine with me," Jane said.

I stared at her with disbelief.

"I . . . why?" I asked.

"I've always liked you," Jane said. "Or I used to, that is. I was around in the fourth grade too, Jenna, remember? We all played together then. Even Liv. I don't think you've really changed that much. The fact that Liv's cut you off proves that."

I looked back and forth at the two of them, Alec solemnly munching on carrot sticks as Jane maintained her level gaze. As I took in Jane's words, it was like she was morphing in front of my eyes. Her hair really wasn't as stringy as I'd thought. Her pale complexion had a delicacy about it. I still had some real doubts about her fashion sense, but my God, was there a pretty face between those feather earrings?

They both looked at me expectantly.

"I feel . . . small," I said finally. Jane grinned sympathetically.

Alec checked his watch.

"You better hurry if you're going to get your teaching in before next period," he said. "Didn't you leave the notes in your locker?" Jane looked startled, and began to eat more quickly.

"I'm supposed to do it after school," she said to me, between bites, "but I'm doing this special thing for Marla—that's the woman I'm reading to for the human-services project."

"What kind of thing?" I asked.

"Oh, it's kind of a long story," Jane replied, finishing

the last of her lunch. "Basically, I'm trying to help her track down one of her cousins she hasn't seen in a million years. The trail has gone pretty cold, but I think I have some leads."

"That's weird," I said, my mind suddenly racing.

"It's not weird," Jane said, sounding hurt.

"No, I didn't mean weird-bad, I meant weird-coincidence. I've been kind of thinking about doing the same thing for mine—for Miss Caples. Maybe finding out where somebody is buried, or something. How would you do that?"

Jane stood up and gathered her things, but she seemed to be considering the question carefully.

"Did the person die in a hospital?" she asked.

"Kind of," I said. "More like an institution."

"That's as good a place to start as any," she said. "Call them. Or send them a letter. I'm really late."

"I'll save you a seat in English Lit," Alec said, and Jane gave him a starstruck look.

"Okay Alec," she said, a little too loudly, and headed for the door.

There was an uncomfortable silence as Alec munched on his lunch, and I watched.

"You're probably not in complete agreement with Jane about forgiving me," I said. He looked up.

"There's nothing to forgive," he said. "You didn't do anything to me. I'm not going to fight Jane's battles for her, she wouldn't want me to," he added.

"I think you behaved like a bitch," he continued, "and

from what I can see, you've more than paid for it. I'm good with that."

I nodded.

"What happened, anyway?" he asked. Then, with a theatrical grin, he added, "Or aren't you the kind that tells?" That was from an old movie, I think.

"I don't know," I said. "If I'm the kind that tells, that is. Or if I was."

I examined my tray.

"Liv wanted me to do something for her," I said finally. "Something awful. And I wouldn't do it. I couldn't. I thought she'd understand, but she didn't."

"She wanted you to do something?" he asked. "Like what?

I just stared at the table.

"It was about Jane, wasn't it?" he said, after a moment.

I nodded.

"She wanted you to do something to Jane, and you refused."

"Yeah," I said softly.

"What was it?" he demanded. I raised my head, and held Alec's look.

"She wanted me to put seventeen dissected frogs in Jane's locker," I said. The color drained from Alec's face.

"You can't be serious," he said.

"I am," I told him.

"She wanted you to kill those frogs anyway, out of

spite, and take Jane's victory away . . . How could a person do that to someone else?"

"I know," I said. "She's gone over the top. Believe me, I realize that. But she didn't actually go through with it. She just thought it up. Nothing really happened, right?"

"She's a lunatic!" Alec muttered.

"She wasn't always like this, Alec," I said. "I know that probably doesn't mean anything to you, and I'm not saying it should, but something is going on with her. She's having, like, problems. At home."

"Yeah, I've heard. Her father's in big trouble, or something."

"I'm not exactly sure," I said. "But yeah, something's going on. And it doesn't make it right, but maybe it explains it a little. And after all, she's too squeamish to do it herself, and I wouldn't do it for her. So don't worry, Alec. I mean, unless she gets her new Big Man to do it for her, you don't–"

"What Big Man?" Alec interrupted.

"You know," I said. "Her new boyfriend."

"Who is . . ." he said, impatiently.

"Clarke Anthony. The football guy."

Alec looked suddenly alarmed.

"I saw him before lunch," he said, "hanging around right near Jane's locker. He had a big box, and he was looking sort of freaked. . . ."

We exchanged startled looks for a moment, then Alec leaped to his feet, knocked his chair over, and dashed for the door. I caught up to him in the hallway, and we raced toward the lockers.

My heart sank as we rounded the corner. I could hear raised voices and shrieks, and I could see a small crowd gathered at the end of the hall. We pushed our way through.

They were everywhere. *Everywhere.*

Frogs.

Chapter 29

The first thing I noticed, with great relief, was that the frogs were alive. And they were literally hopping mad, or more likely just panicked. The next thing I realized was that unless they were all caught, and quickly, more than one was going to end up on the bottom of some-one's shoe. I caught sight of the discarded box on the ground and made a grab for it.

"Alec, here!" I called, pointing to the box. He had a frog in each hand, and was looking around wildly for more. It was almost funny—in fact, it actually was funny, but I refrained from laughing, and kept focused on the task at hand. Alec placed the two frogs in the box, and I quickly closed the lid and looked for another. What with the excited students, and the hysterical shrieks, it was going to be very hard to grab more of them. Holding the box closed, I jumped up onto the windowsill, and shouted at the top of my lungs.

"HEY!!!" I cried, and I was rewarded by a momentary silence, as surprised faces turned to look at me.

"In one half hour," I shouted, "when I'm in Principal Dodson's office telling him how all this happened, I'm going to give him EVERY name of EVERY kid who doesn't leave this hallway in the next ten seconds!!"

"Narc!" a voice called.

"Loser!" called another.

"That's RIGHT!" I shouted. "So I've got absolutely NOTHING to lose when I try to get as many of you detention for the rest of the term as I can! If you don't have anything better to do for the next six Friday afternoons, stick around!" My knees shook the whole time.

There was some more name-calling, and a few helpful suggestions yelled by some of the girls, but the group was definitely moving away. I closed my eyes for a second and tried to still my hammering heart. Thank God Liv hadn't been there. If I'd gone head to head with her, I definitely would have lost.

With the hallway clear, Alec and I spotted a number of the little green critters, and grabbed at them. I looked up when I heard footsteps, and sat back with relief when I saw it was Jane, clutching one of the bio-lab aquariums as she jogged toward us.

"What happened to the mob?" she asked breathlessly, dropping to her knees to scoop up a hopping frog.

"Jenna threatened to name names," Alec said, and Jane shot me a quick, appreciative glance.

"Nice," she said. "I didn't think of that."

"There!" Alec cried, as a small green blur bounced past. I shot a hand out and snagged it, trying not to gag at the undeniable sliminess.

Alec and Jane and I crawled around on the floor for half an hour. In the end, we found fifteen frogs. I thought that was pretty good, considering the pandemonium, but Jane was depressed about the two missing ones.

"They'll turn up, Jane," Alec said, checking the lid of the box to make sure it was secure.

"What are they going to eat?" she asked from the floor, almost in tears. "How are they going to find water?"

Alec and I exchanged a look, and I understood that Jane wasn't to be told what the real plan had been.

As it happened, I did end up in Principal Dodson's office after all. A teacher had happened along during our final scout for the two missing amphibians. I told him only that I assumed it was a trick being played on Jane, and that I'd helped to gather the animals up. To be honest, if I kept the ball rolling by narc-ing and got Liv to retaliate, I was kind of afraid of what she might do next.

On that point, I had to agree with Alec's thinking. Some things it's better just not to know.

Chapter **30**

A full week had passed since the botched frog job. Except for Alec and Jane, no one in my class spoke to me at all. So as soon as the bell rang each day, I made for home as quickly as possible. I began to understand a little bit of what Miss Caples might have felt as the doors of her world slammed shut, one at a time. But she had closed those doors herself.

The universe gives and the universe takes away. Liv was still gone. Out of my sphere. But I had my mother back. It wasn't the same thing, of course. But we did know each other in our own way. Sometimes, she could take one look and know exactly what was going on with me. That can be a little unnerving, but it can also be great. It was wonderful this particular Friday, when I couldn't take the silence any longer, and felt like I just wasn't going to make it through till the end of the day. She showed up just before last period, and told Miss Webster I had a doctor's appointment she'd forgotten about.

"What's going on?" I asked as I climbed into the car.

"Nothing," she said, her hands smoothly clasping the steering wheel. "I just felt like going for a drive, and wanted some company. Do you mind?"

"Mind? I've never been so happy to get out of school in my life!"

"I had a feeling you might need a break today," she said as we pulled out of the parking lot. "Call it mothers' intuition. Want to talk about it?"

I shrugged.

"You know most of it already. Liv wanted me to play this trick on Jane."

"The frog girl."

"Right," I said. "And I told you I had decided to refuse, right?"

She nodded, keeping her eyes on the road.

"So I'm paying for it now. My oldest friend in the whole world has dumped me. And most of my class is, like, completely ignoring me."

"Who are the exceptions?" she asked.

I laughed.

"You'll like this. Jane—the famous frog girl. And Alec. Who's now Jane's boyfriend. The same Alec that got Liv plotting in the first place."

"And you like them?" she asked, casting a quick glance in my direction.

I had already asked myself the same question. Was I sitting with them at lunch only because I simply couldn't do any better? As soon as my mother asked the question, I knew the answer, and it surprised me.

"I do," I said, with a confused smile. "It's totally insane, Mom, but I like them both. I like Jane. I can't explain it. She's the same girl who bugged the hell out of me last month just by being there."

"I'm proud of you, sweetie," she said, after a moment. "Liv really put you to the test, and I think you made the right choice."

"I guess I think so too," I said. "That's pretty much all that makes it bearable. But I still really miss Liv, Mom. Even after everything. And being the class outcast is pretty hard to take."

"It won't last, Jen," my mother said. "I can promise you that. And as for Liv—I'm afraid things probably won't ever be the way they used to be. But most of the other kids will come around. After a few weeks, one or two will forget to ignore you, and then the rest will come back."

"Not Meredith," I said. "Or Amber."

"But you can live without them?" she asked, and I nodded.

"I just don't understand how all this happened," I said. "It wasn't like this last year. Liv never would have asked me to do anything like that. She's so different now. Really mean. And really angry. Why can't she be the way she used to be?"

"She's got a lot going on in her life right now, Jen,"

my mother said. "And no matter what happens, you need to remember that."

"You mean the money thing?" I asked.

"You know, they're losing their house."

"They're selling the house?" I cried.

If you added up all the time I spent in that house, it would be months. Years. Our whole past was in that house. Liv *loved* that house. *I* loved that house.

"The bank is foreclosing and putting it up for sale," she said. "They're going to lose almost everything."

"Is her father going to go to jail?" I asked.

"He's going to have to declare bankruptcy," she said. "But I don't think he'll be going to jail. I think he made some bad business decisions, but he didn't actually do anything criminal. Still, this *is* going to change their lives. You have to be prepared for anything from Liv."

"Why?" I asked.

"Money has always been very important to Liv's parents," my mother said. "I'm sure they passed that same sense of values on to Liv."

"So you mean she feels like she's losing control at home, and has to make up for it by gaining control in school?"

My mother nodded. "Good way to put it," she said.

I remembered asking Liv if she wanted my parents to lend them money, and I cringed.

"Well," I said at last, "at least now I know why I'm an outcast."

"You know, you were too young to realize it, but

when we first moved to Massachusetts, I had a bit of the same problem," my mother said.

"How so?" I asked.

"Fire Hill is a tough town to break into," she said. "For the first six months or so after we moved here, I could barely get a soul to speak to me. There weren't that many younger people here back then, and the older people already had their friends. I was mostly meeting other mothers, picking you up from preschool, and at the playgrounds, and let me tell you, they were a small, icy bunch. And you know who one of the worst was?"

I shook my head.

"Liv's mom," she said, and my eyes widened with surprise.

"It's true," she continued. "You two hit it off right away, and you were always agitating to play together, and visit each other's houses. After some pretty constant toddler whining, Liv's mom would usually give in, but she always made it painfully clear that she wasn't happy about it. She'd only speak to me long enough to get the crucial details out—who'd be at whose house for how long, and who'd drive who home, and that was it. And she never made eye contact with me. The two dads got along okay, though."

"I can't believe it!" I said. "Why didn't you ever say anything to me about it?"

"Well, you were about three at the time, sweetheart. And she loosened up eventually. By the time you were five, she considered me quite acceptable."

"That just amazes me," I said. "I can't believe it."

"People do these things, honey. And I know what's being done to you hurts. But you will get through it. And who knows, a ways down the road you might even be glad it happened."

I opened the window a crack, and let the delicious, chilly smell of autumn into the car. As we drove along a heavily wooded dirt road, I looked up at the tall trees, and thought of our burn-bag. I could almost smell it on the cold breeze blowing onto my face.

Liv had been right about one thing. The past was truly smoke in the wind.

Chapter 31

I had continued walking home each day after school, in spite of the cold, in order to avoid Liv. I'd basically gotten used to her silent animosity in class, and except for a few brief encounters in the locker room, I'd managed to avoid coming into direct contact. As time passed, the idea of being without Liv seemed less devastating, but I still mourned for the lost walks and gossips. Earlier in the day I'd seen her heading for her locker, and for the briefest moment I experienced the familiar jolt of pleasure at seeing her, and felt the impulse to run and tell her how my mother had helped me cut school. Then I remembered.

As far as the rest of the class went, my mother's prediction came true. It seemed two weeks was the limit. Slowly, many of the others began to say good morning, ask me how I was, talk about classes. But for the most part, I chose to continue hanging out with Alec and Jane. They were my friends now. And of course, there was Miss Caples. I looked forward enormously to our weekly visits these days. She had gotten her old camera out to show me, the ancient thing Hannah had given her. I bought her a new one, just the disposable kind, but she seemed really psyched to have it. I had held off telling her about my being Hannah's neighbor, and about the stroke. I was a little afraid of the effect it might have. Maybe she was better off not knowing.

As I approached our driveway, an ambulance, with lights and siren off, turned into Mrs. Madison's driveway. I hurried up to my front door.

"Mom?" I called as I took my coat off and hung it by the door. There was a heavenly smell coming from the kitchen.

"Italian meat pie," my mom said, coming out of the kitchen and gesturing in the direction of the oven.

"It smells amazing. But listen, an ambulance just went up to Mrs. Madison's house."

"Already?" my mother said, crossing to look out the window. "I thought they were waiting until tomorrow," she added.

"I thought you said she couldn't move her arm and couldn't talk," I said.

"She did get some mobility back. She's walking much better now, with help," she explained. "Her right hand is still paralyzed. But with some physical therapy, she'll be able to learn to use her left hand more. She may never be able to speak again, though," she added. "I'm sure there's a nurse with her, but I'll go over after dinner to see how she is."

"Can I come?" I asked.

"Probably not, sweetie," she said. "Let's let her get settled in. I'm sure there will be plenty of opportunities for you to help her later on. Hey, can you set the table?"

Mrs. Madison's house was visible through our kitchen window, and I kept looking up at it as I put the plates and silverware out. I could see a few lights on, which was unusual. I guessed that her nurse would handle everything now. It felt weird even having these semi-concerned thoughts about my old lifelong enemy. I decided I needed to get my mind off it.

"So, Mom, you're not going to *believe* what happened in school today," I said, turning to look at her with a grin.

"I'm *dying* to know," she replied, smiling back. "But there's something I need to get out of the way first. Your dad called today."

I froze, a fork in each hand.

"He had a little proposition to make," she said.

"He's not trying to come back, is he?" I cried, before I could stop myself. I was surprised and relieved when my mother laughed.

"You can put that fear right to bed, Jen," she said. "He wants this divorce to go through at the speed of light. No, it's something else." She looked serious again.

"He wants you to spend Thanksgiving dinner with him."

"No!" I practically shouted, and my mother actually took a step backward.

"Sorry," I said more quietly. "But no. No way. Uh-uh. Forget it. He walked out. He can spend the holidays by himself. I'm with you on Thanksgiving, Mom, and on Christmas, and on Groundhog Day, and Arbor Day, and Canadian Flag Day, and all the rest. There's no negotiating on this, and I'm not going to let him bully me into changing my mind." I gave her a defiant look, and she laughed again.

"You weren't expecting me to argue with you, I hope," she said.

"Well I didn't think so, but . . ." I said.

"Look, Jen, he extended the invitation, so I was obliged to ask. I'll pass on some version of your response to him. But don't close the door on everything. I know you're angry at him, Jen, but you won't be forever. It's different for you. Soon he won't be my husband anymore, but he'll always be your father. Someday, you're going to have to work that out."

I didn't *want* to work it out. I didn't want to think about ever having to *look* at him again.

"Okay," I mumbled. I resisted the urge to cry as I felt her hand gently rub my back.

"So let's eat!" she said.

She took the lid off of the steaming casserole dish, and the most delicious smell in the world escaped in full. The phone rang. My mother made a face.

"I'll say you're not here," I said, reaching for it. I have

a total inability to let a phone ring without answering it. Even pay phones.

"Hello?" I said.

"Jenna? It's Jane."

"Hi!" I said cheerfully. "Any of our web-toed friends turn up today?"

"Still nothing," she replied. "I can't see how they could still be alive after all this time, but Mr. Wood says they're probably fine. Look, I know you're probably about to eat, so I'll be quick. My little brother won a couple of movie passes for next Friday, and he can't go. Interested?"

"Definitely," I said. "What's playing?"

"I'll call and find out," she said. "We can talk about it at school."

"Hey, Jane," I said quickly, feeling she was about to hang up.

"Yeah?" she asked. I didn't even have a question in mind. I just wanted to have a possibly meaningless conversation with a girl my own age on the telephone. I mean, I needed to.

"How did your thing . . . did you find the cousin? For Marla?"

"Oh, not yet," she said. "I'm going to keep at it, though. What about you? Did you find that cemetery?"

"I haven't exactly started trying yet," I said. "Actually, there's more to it than that, now."

I glanced at my mother, who was hovering by the dinner table. She read my expression, and made a little wavy take-your-time-I'll-start-without-you gesture with her hand as she sat down.

"See, there's this other woman Miss Caples knows, who's still alive, but they haven't talked in, like, centuries. And I know where she lives, and everything. The thing is . . . actually, I'm going to have to back up a little bit." And I went way back, to the beginning, and told Jane the whole story of Hattie and Hannah and Julian.

"God, it's like a movie," Jane said when I'd finished.

"I know," I said. "But what do you think? I mean, should I tell her? Or should I just let it go? Mrs. Madison's really sick now. Anything could happen. She could have another stroke and die tomorrow."

"That's exactly why you have to tell Miss Caples right away," Jane said quickly.

"But, why?" I asked.

"You've been given an incredible opportunity, Jen," she said. "Miss Caples has spent hours telling you these stories—clearly these people meant and still mean something to her. Do you want Miss Caples to pick up a newspaper some time and read that Hannah Madison has died? To realize that any chance she had to contact Hannah is now gone forever?"

"She doesn't read the newspaper," I said dumbly.

"You know what I mean," Jane replied gently. "This isn't your choice to make. Miss Caples needs to know, so that *she* can decide what to do."

"You're right. I'll tell her, Jane. I will."

Chapter **32**

It was cold in Miss Caples's apartment. I had gotten a soft blanket out of a trunk, carefully arranged it around her, boiled water for the tea, and dusted the photographs on the coffee table. The latest update on the frogs had been reported. I couldn't stall any longer.

"Uh, Miss Caples?" I asked, without making eye contact.

"Yes, dear?" she said from her chair, looking cozy under the blanket.

"My neighbor across the road, she had a stroke recently."

"Oh my, what a shame," said Miss Caples. "Are you very close to her?"

"Not at all, really," I said. "She was never actually very nice to me. She gets along with my mom some, though. The thing is, Miss Caples, I never knew her first name, actually, at all, until they took her to the hospital. Of course, if I'd heard it before, I probably wouldn't even have remembered–"

"You're rambling ever so slightly, Jenna dear," said Miss Caples with a small smile.

"Her last name is Madison," I said quickly. The smile vanished from her face.

"Not Hannah?"

"Yes, Miss Caples. Hannah Madison. She still lives on Orchard Road. Right across from me."

Miss Caples looked out the window for a moment.

"Thirty-six Orchard Road. That address is burned into my memory," she whispered. "I used to see her car on that road, sometimes."

Suddenly she looked at me sharply.

"A stroke, you said?" I nodded.

"How long has it been since you've seen her?" I asked.

"I've told you that, Jenna. I used to see her at the bank where I worked, but we never spoke. Not since she and I stopped Julian's letters from getting mailed."

"What did you do during all those years after you and Hannah stopped speaking?"

Miss Caples shook her head again.

"I did as little as possible," she said softly. "I kept to myself. At first I kept in touch with some of the St. Mary's Sisters. There had been a time I had seriously considered taking my vows, and joining them there. But after . . . it didn't seem right. I don't know that I was a strong enough person to take those kinds of vows, and frankly, I felt God deserved better. I worked at the bank then, doing mostly secretarial work. I didn't go out much, except to church. Didn't socialize. Didn't really live."

"Why not?" I couldn't help but ask. It was a pushy question, but here Miss Caples was telling me she basically did nothing in her adult life, her incredibly *long* life, but work and sleep. I had to ask.

"Oh, Jenna, you see them in the movies and in books," she began mysteriously. "There's always one somewhere. A mousy, frightened woman. No one seems to know her—who she is or where she lives or what she likes. That's me, Jenna."

"But why?" I asked again, jumping as she pounded her fist on the table.

"Because I was terrified!" she cried. "Always was. I was the most timid little thing you ever wanted to see. I was afraid of everything—cars, influenza, bees, earthquakes. That's one of the reasons I loved Hannah so much—she wasn't afraid of anything! I felt safe with her. For years, I lived through her. But after the Hattie tragedy—when I saw what awful things I was capable of doing, I became afraid of myself, as well."

She laughed suddenly.

"And to think they put Hattie away," she said bitterly. "They should have taken me. I've been afraid of my own shadow for as long as I can remember. But Hattie was really sick, she had a nervous disorder she couldn't control. I had no such excuse. I was just a coward, a coward all my life. I'm a coward now. Sorry you asked?"

"Of course not," I said. "And I *don't* think you're a coward."

"Oh, really?" she asked, looking intently into my eyes. "In what way am I not cowardly, my friend?"

My mind scrambled for an answer.

"But your life isn't over," I said finally. "You could still do something brave."

Miss Caples smiled sadly.

"I appreciate your faith in me, Jenna, but don't get your hopes up. There isn't a brave bone in my body. You want brave, get to know Hannah, your Mrs. Madison. There are a lot of things she isn't and ought to be, but she's braver than a lion, I'll give her that. And to think you live across the street from her. What a world. I can't imagine anything bringing her down. Is it bad? Will she be all right?"

"Well, from what my mom told me, she can't speak at all. And she's mostly paralyzed on her right side."

Miss Caples looked stricken.

"No voice? I couldn't wish that on anyone. Poor, poor Hannah. . . ."

"She may be able to talk again someday," I said, putting my hand over hers. "They just don't know. And my mom said she's having therapy, and she could regain some use of her right hand. Until then, the nurse is doing everything she needs."

Miss Caples didn't say anything.

"Should I not have told you? Did I make a mistake? I just thought—"

Miss Caples silenced me with one raised hand. She looked deep in thought.

"This means something," she said, finally. "It cannot be an accident that I've dwelled so heavily on my misdoings these past several weeks. And now this news of Hannah. What can it mean?"

"Miss Caples?" I said. "Maybe it means . . . I don't know, that you're meant to get in touch with Hannah again or something. To talk about what happened."

Miss Caples was shaking her head no with such force, her hair was coming loose from its bun.

"No, no, that's out of the question," she said.

"Out of the question?" I asked. Miss Caples didn't seem to want to look at me all of a sudden.

"No," she said again. "I can't change who I am. I'm too old. I've made my choices."

"But, I mean, why not try just once?" I pressed. "You could just call her—well, actually I guess you couldn't call her, since she can't talk. But you could go and see her, maybe, she only lives a few minutes away, and I'm sure my mom would drive—"

"Jenna, please, I said no!" Miss Caples cried fiercely.

But I *couldn't* let it go.

"I need to know why," I said in a low, determined voice.

"If you'd been listening, you'd already know," she said.

"You're afraid," I said suddenly. And I realized that

her fear was the one thing I couldn't argue with. But maybe she'd be willing to start with a smaller, safer step.

"Okay," I said. "I have another idea. Something different. You said something once about wishing you knew how Hattie died, and where she was buried. Remember?"

"Yes," she replied.

"Well, what about contacting WindHill? Maybe there's someone there who remembers Hattie. You wouldn't even have to call, if you didn't want to. You could write them a letter. I'm sure their address is in the book."

There was a long pause, and I wasn't sure she'd heard anything I said. Then she took a deep breath.

"I think I can do that," she said. "I think I'd like to. If I write them a letter, you'll mail it for me?"

"Of course," I said, surprised and sort of tickled by the determination on her face.

"It wouldn't be much, but it would be something," she said. "To know. Perhaps you could put some flowers on her grave. Light a candle in the chapel."

"I'd be happy to," I said.

"Well?" she said, taking a look around the room. "I suppose we ought to start with a paper and a pen."

One small step for Miss Caples.

Chapter **33**

My mother finally decided it would be okay for me to go to Mrs. Madison's house to help. Mom had been cooking Mrs. Madison dinner and bringing it over to her almost every night. I felt oddly nervous as my mother wrapped the steaming plate in tin foil.

"Ready?" she asked, then saw from my face that I wasn't.

"What is it, Jen?"

"It's just . . ." I faltered. "What should I say? How should I act?"

"Just be your normal self," my mother replied. "And remember to look at Mrs. Madison when you speak to her. Be natural."

"Okay," I said, my doubts sounding clearly in my voice.

"Honey, would you rather not come?" she asked.

Definitely. But I knew I had to go. Mrs. Madison had been like a generic evil cartoon character, all of my life. Given what I now knew, somehow I felt I owed it to her, and in a weird way to Miss Caples, to finally face her and try to view her in a new light.

"Let's go," I said.

I held the steaming plate in both hands as my mother slipped her key into Mrs. Madison's door. The key turned with a grinding noise in the lock, and the door swung inward. Just a few steps, and I was inside Mrs. Madison's house. *Terra Incognita.*

What I saw surprised me. Unlike the decay and disrepair of the house's exterior, its inside was immaculate. I peered into a room to the right of the door. The furniture, rugs, and lamps were arranged with style. I was surprised by its brightness. The whole room looked completely unlived in, with no personal mementos or touches that usually make a home look like it belongs to somebody. I glanced into another room across the hall. This one was a small sitting room with a fireplace. There was the same almost military neatness and order.

"I never imagined it would be like this," I whispered to my mother.

"I was surprised too," my mother said.

She led me past a grand staircase.

"They moved her down here to the first floor," my mother explained. "Mrs. Madison?" she called. "It's Grace, from across the street. I've brought my daughter, and we have your dinner."

I heard a creak, and a dark-haired woman in a white uniform appeared in the hallway.

"Oh hello, Jerilyn," Mom said. "How is she today?"

"Sleeping like a rock right now," the nurse replied. "She's been cranky today, though. A real spitfire. That's a good sign."

"Glad to hear it," said my mother.

"You can go on in," Jerilyn said. "Just leave the plate on the side table, and she'll wake to that nice smell. Maybe that'll pick up her appetite a bit."

"Thank you, Jerilyn," Mom said. "Ready, Jen?"

I nodded and followed my mother down the hallway. She turned into the last room on the left. Just inside the door was a wheelchair, looking lonely and unused. I stared at it for a moment, recognizing the familiar smell permeating the room—that unmistakable hospital smell. As my mother crossed the room, I looked toward the bed.

Mrs. Madison was indeed fast asleep. Her bed was an actual hospital bed, the big, bulky kind that can be adjusted automatically. She lay propped up on several pillows, her hair, nearly colorless, down and hanging about her face. The sight of her pinched face gave me a jolt. She looked ancient. The stroke had really taken its toll. Seeing how thin and tiny she appeared on that big bed, I felt a sudden pang of sadness. This was no way to end up. No matter what Mrs. Madison had done, or who she'd been, she didn't deserve this.

A bag hanging from the bed caught my attention. It was filled with liquid, and I had a brief and bizarre sense that it contained apple juice being pumped directly into her veins. Then I realized exactly what it was. I guess Mrs. Madison was now too feeble to get to the bathroom. It was probably a great help for her not to have to go. But that didn't stop me from feeling that it was a terrible thing, after living almost ninety years of independence, to have to pee in a bag.

Mrs. Madison moved then, shifting clumsily. I took a step back, and a floorboard creaked underfoot. I had looked away, but now I glanced back at the bed and felt a little shudder begin in my spine. Mrs. Madison was looking at me. Her eyes were red and glassy, her mouth opened in a silent *O*. She worked her lips for a moment, as if she was trying to speak. I felt the impulse to turn away, but something made me hold her gaze. I wanted to say her name, Hannah. But I didn't. Then her eyes closed again.

I muttered something to my mother about getting some fresh air, and rushed out of the house. The door slammed behind me, and I sat down on the front steps, breathing deeply. I drew as much of the cool, sweet evening air as I could into my lungs and held it there, savoring the feeling.

Chapter **34**

I had just stepped into Miss Caples's living room when she began waving an envelope at me.

"They wrote back!" she said, her eyes shining. "And it's *quite* astonishing what they have to say."

"Tell me!" I said, pulling up a chair.

"They gave my letter to a senior nurse, who began working at WindHill the year before Hattie died. She remembers Hattie, and says she grew quite close to her. She writes that Hattie was very well liked, and had many friends. This same nurse was with Hattie when she died, quietly, of heart failure."

"Then she wasn't alone," I said. "See? Aren't you glad you found out?"

Miss Caples nodded, and said, "But there's more. Listen to this."

She opened the letter and began to read.

". . . and I recall quite clearly where Hattie is buried—in a corner plot in the little cemetery behind the old St. Mary's School. I attended the funeral with many of Hattie's friends from WindHill. There is quite a lovely headstone that her friend picked out. She took care of all the funeral arrangements, just as she had taken care of Hattie's expenses over the years. She never came to visit, but I believe her name was Madison."

"Hannah?" I gasped.

"My Hannah," she replied, her eyes gleaming.

"But, I don't understand," I said. "I thought Hannah hated Hattie. Why would she take care of her bills? Why would she arrange for her funeral and headstone?"

Miss Caples shook her head slowly.

"I cannot imagine, Jenna. It seems there are more pieces to this puzzle. Something must have happened to make Hannah change her mind about Hattie, or feel responsible for her. But what?"

"Maybe after a few years she started to feel sorry for what she'd done. She might have wanted to make it up to her."

"Maybe," said Miss Caples, but she didn't look as if she thought so.

"I saw her, you know," I said suddenly. I hadn't meant to say anything, but then there it was.

"Saw Hannah?" she asked, and I nodded.

"How did she look?"

I opened my mouth to reply, but no sound came out. I felt the sting of warm tears in my eyes, and I bit on my lower lip to stop them from coming. Miss Caples looked at me, then turned and looked out the window for a long time.

"There is something you can do for me, if you have the time," she said finally.

"Of course!" I said. "Anything. What is it, Miss Caples?"

She fixed me with a determined stare.

"Help me on with my coat."

"Your coat?" I asked. I didn't even know she had one.

She nodded grimly. "I can't do it alone, but perhaps we can do it together. It's time," she said, getting to her feet, "that I went outside."

Chapter 35

I leaned my head against my locker, exhausted from the previous week's events. Frankly, getting Miss Caples outside by myself seemed a bit more than I could handle. It had come as a great relief when Miss Caples had agreed to let my mother help out. On the first try, with Mom on one side and me on the other, we walked as far as the driveway. Miss Caples had stared wide-eyed, looking almost wild with fright. Mom was great, though. She kept up a constant, natural-sounding chatter that distracted us all. Before we knew what was happening, we were back in the front hallway, the door safely closed behind us. Only then did Miss Caples release the white-knuckled grip she'd had on my forearm.

We started all over again the next afternoon, and made slight but definite progress. The third day we walked almost an eighth of a mile down the road. The fourth day, even farther. Miss Caples never gave an explanation for her sudden determination. I sensed that something had suddenly kicked into motion inside her. I didn't know where it would lead her but for now, the action itself was enough.

I heard footsteps, and looked up to see Alec coming toward me with a big grin on his face.

"Guess what?" he asked, and before I could answer, he opened his hands to show me a small frog cowering inside.

"Hopped right past Ellis Green in social studies. She almost passed out. Sixteen down, one to go!"

"It's okay?" I asked. "After all this time?"

"See for yourself," he said, grinning. "The little guy looks in the pink of health. Or the green, anyway."

"That's great, Alec," I said.

"Jane is going to be so psyched," he said.

"Jane is going to be psyched about what?" came a voice from behind me.

Alec raised the frog triumphantly in front of Jane.

"You found number sixteen!" she cried. "Is he all right? Did you give him some water?"

"He's fine, Jane," Alec said. "I'm going to keep him in the lab aquarium until after school, then I'll let him go in the pond where we put the others."

"You're keeping him in the bio lab?" I asked. "Kind of ironic, isn't it? I hope they're not discussing animal guts today. You might traumatize him."

I was joking, but I was also surprised at the feeling of relief I had upon seeing the frog.

"How's it going with Miss Caples?" Jane asked.

"Well, yesterday we went almost to the Town Hall and back. That's about a half mile, I think. So she's really cruising."

"That's awesome, Jenna," said Jane. "You should be really proud of yourself. Most people around here have been whining since day one about this human-services project."

"Well . . ." I said. "I wasn't exactly jazzed about it in the beginning."

"But you are now," she said. "And you're getting Miss Caples jazzed too."

I smelled Liv's perfume before I heard her.

"Plotting an overthrow of the Home Ec department?" she said. "Planning on converting school lunches to vegetarian?"

I turned to look at her, and was stabbed by the feelings that still surfaced. There were things I wanted to say, things I could have said. But I decided to try Jane's approach, and didn't rise to the bait.

"I see the pond squatter disease has spread," Liv said, glancing at the frog peeking out of Alex's hands, then looking me up and down. "So you're keeping company with reptiles these days?"

"Amphibians, actually," I said. "And we've got sixteen of them back, so far. All but one, happily, and we'll find that one too."

Liv looked at Alec and Jane, and rolled her eyes. "You don't even have sense enough to be embarrassed, do you, Jen?"

"I'm not embarrassed," I said. "And neither are my friends."

"Your friends?" she said, with an exaggerated laugh.

"Yes, her friends," said Alec, looking intently at her.

Liv probably would have said something nasty if Jane or I had spoken. But with Alec, she shut her mouth.

"Whatever," she finally said, turning her back on us.

"It's crazy," I said, as she walked away. "But after everything that's happened, after everything she's done, I still miss her sometimes."

"She was your best friend for a really long time," said Jane. "You can't just turn that off."

Too true, I thought, sadly realizing that I was the only one who wanted to try and get back what we'd once had.

Chapter 36

"I'm afraid I don't have anything planned for dinner," my mother said. "I just dropped Miss Caples off, and it took longer than I thought."

"Dropped Miss Caples off?" I said, feeling frightened. "What happened to her? Is she all right? Why didn't you call me?"

"Jen, it's fine! There's nothing the matter with her. Sweetheart, I thought she'd have mentioned it to you."

"Mentioned what?" I asked, still feeling fear in the pit of my stomach. She's sick, I thought. And she didn't want me to know.

"She wanted to visit Mrs. Madison. She asked me to drive her there. Didn't I hear you telling Jane they hadn't spoken for decades?"

My mouth opened and closed, fishlike.

"Jenna? You look dumbfounded."

A good way to put it. I shook my head.

"Wait. Miss Caples went to see Mrs. Madison? When?"

"I just told you, sweetheart. She called me this morning, after you'd left for school, and asked me to drive her there. I picked her up after lunch, and dropped her at Mrs. Madison's. And drove her home afterward."

"But that just doesn't make any sense," I muttered.

"What doesn't, Jen?" she asked. "Is there something more to this? Something I should know?"

"Not really," I said. "It's true that Miss Caples hadn't spoken to Hannah, to Mrs. Madison, in years. She told me all about it. I'm just surprised that she'd decide to go see her without saying anything to me."

"Well, it did sound like something of an impulse, when she called," my mother said. "Carpe diem."

"Seize the day," I translated automatically. "I guess Miss Caples has seized the day. God. It's about time."

Chapter **37**

I was practically exploding with impatience as Miss Caples slowly poured herself a cup of tea, then another one for me.

"Milk? Sugar?" she asked, and I shook my head almost frantically. I had the distinct impression Miss Caples was enjoying herself.

"Well then," she said, settling back in her chair, cupping the tea between her hands. "We've had quite a week, haven't we?"

"Miss Caples, *come on!* I know you went to see Hannah. What's going on? Why didn't you tell me?"

She looked serious for a moment.

"I should have told you, Jenna. You're a part of this now, and I should have told you. But I honestly didn't know if I could go through with it until I actually did. I had the idea a week ago, when I asked you to take me outside. I hoped I would be strong enough. I didn't want to disappoint you. And to be honest, I wanted to see if I could do it by myself."

"And you did!" I said, giving her arm an encouraging pat.

"I certainly did," she said, looking pleased.

"So? What happened?

"Well, it was not a tearful and joy-filled reunion," Miss Caples said. "The nurse said Hannah had agreed to see me, but for quite a while she refused to even acknowledge I was there. Heavens, she looks terrible, doesn't she?"

I nodded.

"So I talked to her instead. About you. About my life, which didn't take long. And I told her about the nurse at WindHill. About Hattie's headstone, and that I knew who'd paid for it. And that's when she finally looked at me. It was a long, hard look."

She paused as her cat leapt off her lap.

"Hannah can only communicate through writing on a pad, and only then with her left hand. So it took a while for her to put it on paper, but I have an idea now of what happened. You and I liked to think maybe Hannah had changed her mind about Hattie, or felt remorse, but it wasn't so. No, it was Julian who did it."

"Julian?" I asked.

"Yes. Before he left for the war in Spain, Hannah explained, he made her take a vow. If anything should happen to him, he said, Hannah must swear to look after Hattie. To take care of her needs. And as much as Hannah disapproved of and maybe still hated Hattie, she truly loved Julian. So she promised to do as he asked. When Julian was killed, Hannah made good on that promise."

"So she did it for Julian," I said, taking it all in.

"Yes," Miss Caples said. "Hannah didn't write anything else to me after that. We just sat silently for a while, and finally I got up to go. I was opening the front door when her nurse caught up with me. She gave me a box. Something she said Mrs. Madison had her get down from a closet."

"What was it?" I asked.

Miss Caples reached down beside her chair and picked up an old steel box, which she placed on her lap. She opened it, and I leaned forward to get a better look.

In the box was a stack of delicate, yellowing rectangles of paper. They were covered with spidery scrawl.

"Letters?" I asked, and Miss Caples nodded, her eyes wide.

"Not . . . but they're not those letters, are they? Julian's letters to Hattie?"

"The same," she said. "All here." She took the letters out of the box, and ran her hands over them.

"But why would she have saved them?" I asked. "They were love letters to Hattie. Why did she keep them?"

"Because Julian wrote them," she said. "And he was gone forever. That's why she kept them."

I sifted through the letters, almost afraid they would

disintegrate at my touch. "Did you . . . did you read them?"

"Not really," Miss Caples said. "That would be too painful. And too private. But I did look through the envelopes, and I found something."

She removed the bottom letter from the pile and held it up to show me. The envelope looked different, and there were many more stamps.

"What is it?" I asked.

"This is Julian's last letter to Hattie," she told me. "It was written much later. It's postmarked from Spain. This one, he mailed himself. It is the only letter we can be certain Hattie definitely read. And it is the only letter I read, as well."

"What does it say?"

"He told her that he would come back to her after the war. That he was sorry that she had not responded to his letters, but that he understood her wish for privacy. That he wished to tell her one last time that he loved her, and hoped she might one day love him again."

"Then she knew," I said. "All those years, in WindHill, she did know that Julian had loved her, and would've waited for her."

"Yes," Miss Caples said. "And I take enormous comfort from that fact. It doesn't change what I did, or completely relieve my burden, but it does help to know."

"But how did Hannah get this letter?" I asked.

"Hattie had no next of kin," Miss Caples said. "I suppose as Hattie's benefactor, her personal possessions were sent to Hannah after her death."

"Well then, maybe that included all of them," I said, looking at the stack of envelopes.

"All of them?"

"Don't you think Hannah might have finally delivered the letters to Hattie after making the promise to Julian? As part of that promise? Maybe she did, and she got them all back, plus the last one, when Hattie died."

I fingered the pile of yellowing envelopes.

"These have been opened," I said. "Somebody read them. It could have been Hattie."

"I suppose we'll never know that," said Miss Caples.

"You could ask Hannah the next time you see her."

"I don't know if there will be a next time," replied Miss Caples. "It took a great deal of effort to make a very small step with Hannah. Clearly she didn't want me there. This may be as far as Hannah and I go."

"But she gave you the box of letters," I said. "Why would she have done that if she didn't want to see you again?"

"I suppose even Hannah feels the need to make some kind of amends," she said. "With the stroke, she's feeling her own mortality. She can't have much time left. Sometimes people feel the need to set things right, to the best of their ability, when they feel their time is near."

Miss Caples looked at me for a long time, then reached down beside her chair and rummaged about for something.

"Don't move," she said.

When she straightened in her chair again, I saw that

she was holding the little disposable camera I'd given her.

"Smile," she said, and the flash made a tiny pop. Then she sat back deeply in her chair, her hands wrapped around the camera. Just beyond her, hanging on the wall, the black-and-white faces of Hannah, Hattie, and Julian came suddenly into focus.

Chapter **38** *Elspeth*

Time seems to have stopped somehow. Or perhaps, like a stop-watch, it's simply come full circle, and is beginning again. I still see the three of us as girls. Am I crazy? One dead over thirty years, one mute, and a third who only gets out once a decade or so. But I feel as if we're merely playing dress-up, or spooking for sport on Halloween. Young faces and minds gig-gling behind wrinkled dime-store costumes. What masks we have crafted for ourselves. What fantasies do they create that weren't there all along? What do they hide that couldn't be seen from the beginning?

I have lived almost nine decades. I have done shameful things in my life, and I have hidden myself away from the world, but perhaps at long last I can truly say that I am not afraid. I have glimpsed courage, and it has nourished me. Never again will I allow that fear to bind my arms at my sides.

I will spend the rest of my days living with what I've done. I will not let a single one pass without thinking of Hattie and Julian. I will visit Hannah again. And every night, before I go to sleep, I will think just briefly of the light I took from Hattie. But I will also think of the light she kept inside her, through the darkness. I will kindle that light in me, and watch it grow. For however long I have left.

Jenna says she will continue to come and see me, though her school program ends after Christmas. She has even promised to take me to church on Sundays. Sweet child. What is it about youth? Real youth? Such poison and passion, dancing and wrestling all at once. Jenna's passion has changed my life. Perhaps my role in this will recompense her for the service she has done for me. She seems well enough, without her friend. And who knows what lies ahead? Perhaps those two will find each other again, and make things right. Stranger things have happened.

I don't know if this is peace. I don't know if it is ever going to be peace. But if it never gets any better than this, I can truly say I will not be unhappy. And if the past grows too heavy, here in this old apartment, I have simply to walk down to Orchard Road, where the past meets the future. Jenna is young and strong and ready to plunge into the world. I have had my taste of those waters too. I wish her all that I could not give myself. For Hattie, for Julian, for Hannah, and for me. Peace. Strength. Courage.

Life.

Chapter 39

Alec rode in circles around the driveway as Jane folded her bike's kickstand.

"Thanks for lunch. Your mom's the greatest cook. And what an amazing story, Jen," she said. "You know, if you'd just read to her like Miss Webster said, none of this would have happened."

"Well, I guess a little rule-breaking now and then is a good thing," I said.

"I can hardly disagree with that," Jane said with a smile.

"Jaaaane," Alec called.

"Coming!" she called back. "I gotta hop. Next time we'll do this at my house, okay?"

"Hey," I said, grabbing her bike for a moment. "Jane, listen. Thanks. You know. For everything."

She gave me a big smile. "Anytime, girlfriend," she said.

I let go of the bike, and she sped off to join Alec at the bottom of our driveway. I walked down the driveway behind them, slowly. When I got to the bottom, Jane and Alec had already disappeared over the hill. I saw a lone figure walking toward me.

Liv saw me right away, but she didn't say anything. I didn't say anything either, just watched her walk by. I'd seen the moving van in front of her house. She'd probably be gone before the day was out. When she was about twenty feet past our driveway, she suddenly called out over her shoulder.

"There isn't a seventeenth."

"What?" I called back. She stopped for a moment, and turned to face me.

"There were only sixteen frogs. You got them all."

There was so much distance between us, I couldn't see her face that well, or tell if she wanted to say more.

"Okay," I called.

"I just thought you'd want to know that," she said, and then she continued on her way.

"Thanks," I said softly, probably too softly for her to hear. I watched her for just a moment, and then I looked across the street at Mrs. Madison's house. It still looked shoddy and decrepit, but I knew the real story now, or some of it. For years, I had just assumed Mrs. Madison had always been the sour, bad-tempered old lady who so harassed me. I had never bothered to think of her as a real person, to give her the benefit of the doubt in that small way. And in the beginning, I had looked at Miss Caples the same way. But Miss Caples had given me a great gift. She *listened* to me. And in listening, gently offered up her own past. With each story, each photograph she shared, she gave me a piece of herself, and of Julian, Hattie, Hannah, and even myself.

There is a new photograph in Miss Caples's apartment, the first addition in a half-century. I was looking straight at her as she snapped it, and there is a small smile on my face, puzzled but affectionate.

I feel honored to have been added to Miss Caples's story. And I'm glad that she is allowing herself room in her life for new memories and moments. It seems ages have passed since I first rang Miss Caples's doorbell, tentatively opened the door, looked into her life, and looked again.